The Floor of the World

Other Books by Charles Ott:

Something Made of Vacuum
An SF Romantic Comedy

A Weapon of Mathematics
A Fantasy Adventure

The Floor of the World

by Charles Ott

Table of Contents

Chapter 1

Portal of Praise church on the South side of Chicago was rocking when Peter Wiegand stepped cautiously through the heavy wood doors into the chapel. It felt as though it were *literally* rocking: the wooden floor thrummed with the music. He moved to stand against the back wall of the sanctuary in front of a stained-glass window and watched the choir, twenty rows of pews away, stepping back and forth and clapping, while a grinning teenage drummer whaled away on his traps and a guitarist and bassist joined in behind them. They were singing "He's An On-Time God" and the congregation clapped their hands high and stepped from side to side in their pews, singing along.

Wiegand was the only white person in the building.

A fat black woman in an elaborate hat came up to him, and they bent down a little to talk as though it were possible to get below the music. "Hi!" she said, not quite whispering. "Welcome to this house! What's your name?"

"Peter Wiegand."

"I beg your pardon?"

"WYE-gand."

"I meant your first name."

"Oh. Pete."

"Pete!" she said. "I'm Delores. We're glad you're here! We'll make a place for you and you just sit down and feel the spirit." She led him to a pew and made vague shooing motions to the people there. They

1

stepped left and didn't step right again, still singing, and left a place for him at the end.

"I'm here to pick up a friend of mine," Wiegand said, as though an explanation were required.

He sat down and Delores crouched in the aisle next to him, bracing herself on the arm of the pew. "Who's that?" she asked.

"Brian Covington."

"Little Brian? He's in the choir. You can see him later, we're running a little late today. You enjoy yourself, now. God loves you and we do, too." She moved away.

"He may not come when you want Him, but He'll be there right on time! He's an on-time God, yes He is!" they sang. Wiegand stood and looked for a hymnal, then noticed that no one else was using one. He tried clapping along with the beat but it didn't work. He settled for swaying vaguely back and forth, clapping his hands so tentatively that no one could hear.

Summer sunlight, as rich as olive oil, flooded through the yellow stained-glass windows in the church. The sanctuary was built massively of brown brick. The building dated from the 1890's, and the texts in the windows were in German.

Whatever the congregation was feeling, clearly the choir members were having a grand time, grinning and laughing. Brian Covington was easily visible on the back riser. He was six feet tall and his manic grin and up-brushed hair seemed to float over the choir. He spotted Wiegand's face — not a difficult thing — and waved while singing, then hit a downbeat on his tambourine with a smack so tremendous Wiegand wondered how he could do it without hurting his hand.

Presently the song came to an end, with many flourishes from the musicians, but nobody sat down. Wiegand looked around uncertainly, bent his legs a little, then stood back up. Apparently everyone else could recognize some body language cues from the choir that he didn't see, because the drummer rattled off an opening, one of the men pulled out a harmonica and they launched into "He Ain't Never Done Me Nothin' But Good."

This was even dancier than the last song, and Wiegand felt hopelessly out of place. He swayed and flapped his hands, his eyes a little desperate.

The song eventually ended and the congregation sat. The preacher stepped forward to the pulpit. However, the choir members, who had started to sit down, apparently still had some music left in them. Some of the women in the first row started up one of the verses again — "I won't repent, I won't recant, tell me why I should?" The men in the back row joined in and by the time the chorus came around the whole choir was back on their feet, singing "He ain't never done me nothin', never done me nothin' but good!"

The congregation stood again, with Wiegand a little behind everyone else, and they clapped and sang louder than before.

They came to the end a second time. The preacher stood again, grinning, and asked the choir "You guys are all done now, right? I can finish up?"

"Amen!" said a few of the women in the choir. "Preach it, Reverend!"

"Please rise for the benediction," the pastor said, his voice resonant, and everyone stood again, quietly this time. "From the letter of Paul to the Romans: May the God of endurance and encouragement grant you to live in such harmony with one another, in accord with Christ Jesus, that together you may with one voice glorify the God and Father of our Lord Jesus Christ."

"Amen!" the congregation said, and the service was over.

The choir slipped out to the side, pulling off their scarlet and white robes as they went. Wiegand left his pew to avoid blocking the other people, and returned to stand under a golden window with his back to the wall. Delores found him again and came up to give him a hug. "Pete, you must be one of Brian's friends from the college, right? Did he ask you pick him up after service?"

"Yeah, we have some work to do on our project," Wiegand said.

"Well, usually the service is over by now. We're just kind of behind today. We're sure glad you came, though. Come on downstairs, we've got doughnuts and stuff, and anyway that's where little Brian will be."

"Little Brian?"

An older woman came up and reached out her arms to Wiegand for a hug also. "Hi, I'm sister Corelle," she said. "Yeah, ain't that something? We still call him Little Brian even when we're standing looking up at him. He was in my first Sunday school class here, when he actually was little."

Another white-haired woman mentioned, "He was always a smart kid."

Corelle laughed. "He was a little motor-mouth, that one. We used to put him in the cloakroom to get him to stop talking, and he'd keep going all by himself in there."

"He still talks fast," Wiegand said with a little grin.

"We're all proud of him," Delores said. "He did real good with his education."

"I hope he brought back my CDs and movies," another woman said, and added, "Your name's Pete? Pete, you come back and see us sometime when you can stay for the whole service, okay?"

"Um, sure," Wiegand said. "Hey, I've got some of the discs that Brian borrowed out in my car. Let me go get them, it'll be just a minute."

"Okay, then come on downstairs for coffee and fat pills!"

"Yeah," a man passing by remarked. "Y'all been takin' them fat pills."

"You ought to know," Corelle said cheerfully. "We gotta fight past you to get them."

Wiegand stepped gratefully through the doors, down the front steps and around to the sunlit quiet of the parking lot. His shabby blue Ford had the windows an inch open to keep the interior from getting so hot it would damage the two shopping bags full of music CDs and movie DVDs. The discs, with and without plastic "jewel boxes," were wrapped with grocery bags and rubber bands into smaller packages. He unlocked the car doors and took out the shopping bags, relocked the car and stood for a moment, breathing deeply, before he turned to go back inside.

The pastor had reached the front door now to greet the people as they left. Wiegand was obliged to shake his hand, relate the story of being a friend of Brian's from "the college", and get more hugs and handshakes. Finally he was able to get past the knot of people at the door and go downstairs to the basement, where the noise level was even higher than before.

The basement had a low ceiling with recessed fluorescent lights, and green-painted walls decorated with Sunday-school posters. Covington was pouring himself a cup of coffee from an urn at the far end. When he stood up with the coffee, he was a full head higher than the people around him, even counting the ladies' hats. Wiegand ducked and weaved through the crowd and made his way the length of the basement to deposit the bags in front of him.

"Hey, Pete! Sorry we were running late!" Covington said. "Have some coffee. Have a doughnut."

"Have a cookie," one of the women said. "We got lots."

A tiny black girl, no more than four and with braids decorated with shiny metalized plastic bows, toddled over to Wiegand and looked up at him. "You're a white person," she said. "Like on TV."

"Yes, I am," Wiegand said, entirely at a loss.

"Are you on TV?"

"No, I'm afraid not."

"Oh." The girl lost interest and wandered off.

"Sister Ann," Covington said to a short, gray-haired woman in a broad white hat, "I've got your discs to give back." He fished in the paper bags and pulled out a stack of DVDs bound with rubber bands, with a scrap-paper label on top.

She accepted them and said, "Little Brian, I loaned you these because it's you, but you're not making bootleg copies, are you? That wouldn't be right."

"No, no, they're for our project at school. Sister Ann, everybody, this is my friend Pete. He's a computer guy, one of the other postdocs, and he's doing the software for us. Pete, this is Ann. She's related to me — it's kind of complicated."

"Hello, how are you?" Wiegand said shyly and quickly stuck out his hand for a handshake, to forestall a hug.

The old woman shook his hand graciously. "I'm blessed!" she said. "It's nice to meet you. Brian doesn't bring people from his college over very often. So you're a programmer and Brian is doing ... what?"

For a moment, the chatter in the basement dropped to silence. In an instant the noise resumed, as everybody began speaking at once. "That was weird," Covington said. "I guess that happens every once in a while, like at a party where everybody stops talking by coincidence, but it's never happened with this many people that I can remember."

Wiegand's eyes were wide. "It wasn't that," he said. "I saw something."

"What did you see?"

"Uh ... later."

"Okay," Covington said, then turned back to Sister Ann. "Anyway, my part of the project, I designed the cooling system," he said.

"I thought you were a chemist," she said.

"I'm in materials science," Covington said. "Sort of like a chemist. Better, if you want my opinion."

Two other women came up and said hello all around, and Covington handed them both packages of discs. "Hi, I'm Tianna," one said to Wiegand. "Help us out to understand here, will you? We keep asking Brian but we don't get any sense out of him. I loaned Brian what I had at home, which is " — she flipped through the discs in her hand — "a whole bunch of Disney movies my kids used to like, a set of old *Amos 'n Andy* shows that my grandma wanted to watch, some good gospel music, some really nasty music my boys don't know I took away from them and which they are *not* getting back, some video games, and I don't know what this one is. What are you doing with all this stuff?"

Wiegand answered, more sure of himself now that he was on familiar ground. "We're part of a group building a new computer memory chip, with a lot more density than anybody ever had before. It holds ... well, it holds a lot. I want to load it up with all different content, so I've been borrowing digital discs from my friends and Brian does the same. Then we have a sort of robot jukebox player that loads them all into the system, plus we have the biggest honkin' fiber-optic internet pipe you ever saw, and some other input channels. Anyway, after the discs are all loaded up we can give them back to you. And thanks from me, too, by the way. I appreciate you loaning us all this."

"So it's like a big Tivo?" Tianna asked.

"If you had a Tivo like this," Covington laughed, "you'd have the coolest home theater system on the block. You could record every TV show on every channel."

"At minus 321 Fahrenheit," Wiegand said, "that would be a *really* cool Tivo. If I had a home theater system like that, I could get a girlfriend."

"If you had a girlfriend who was impressed by minus 321 Fahrenheit, she'd probably be frigid," Covington said.

"Pete, Brian! Stop it right now! What do you mean?" Ann asked.

Covington jumped in. "He means the chip has a liquid-nitrogen cooling system I built. My part of the project is to get rid of the heat from the chip, so we put it on this really advanced engineered copper substrate with nano-sized channels with terrific thermal conductivity, and then the liquid-nitrogen plumbing sucks the heat out and wastes it to the air, but the system is pretty fussy and I like to get in every day to look at it, even Sunday."

"Same ol' Brian," Tianna said. "He stopped making sense a long time ago. Pete, I'm still wondering why you want old movies and gospel music."

"I just need a lot of different content. I need to fill up the chip to test it," Wiegand said. "We're still trying to figure out how much it will actually hold."

"I thought you did a capacity test already," Covington said. "Couple-three weeks ago."

"Yeah, but that was just DEADBEEF," Wiegand said. The others looked at him blankly, and he added, "A hex test pattern. To get a real test, I have to load it with real data. I have an indexing routine that looks at everything coming in and rejects anything that's already there, so when we reach capacity we'll know it's all different data."

"All movies and music?"

"Oh, God no," Wiegand said, then caught himself. "Sorry. I mean, no. It's anything I could get. I got the librarian at school to give me a big old hand-truck full of cardboard boxes of discs, like a complete run of, you know, *The Journal of Sedimentary Mineralogy* from 1992 to date or something. We threw all of that into the chip, too. Plus whatever comes in on that internet pipe, all kinds of stuff. It's all data, and all indexed."

Another moment of silence descended on the crowd, and was gone in an instant.

"Again everybody stops talking? Something funny is going on today," Tianna said.

Ann said, "Amen to that. Boys, we have to go. Brian, is your mama here today?"

"Yeah, she's over by the classroom there."

"Okay, I need to go talk to her. Pete, you come back and see us. Remember, this isn't our house, it's God's house, and you're part of the family."

"Well, thanks," Wiegand said. Ann and the others walked away and Covington turned anxiously toward him.

"I saw it that time," Covington said. "Kind of like a ripple or a refraction. It came in the north wall and went through the hall."

"I'm glad you saw it too. That's what I saw," Wiegand said. "A little twinkle in the light. You got any ideas?"

"Not a clue," Covington said.

Wiegand began, "We ought to ...", then was silent.

"I know what you mean," Covington said. "But ... tell you what, let's get back to the lab and we'll do what we always do. Look it up on the internet."

"Okay," Wiegand said immediately. "Are you about ready to go?"

"Oh, relax, Pete. You look like somebody's gonna sneak up and baptize you from behind."

"Somebody's likely to run up and give me a hug," Wiegand said darkly. "We didn't do that back in my church, when I was a kid. Church isn't my scene anyway."

"Chill, dude. These are my people, they're all pretty nice."

"Usually when I'm in a church, somebody died or somebody's getting married," Wiegand said. "I'm just nervous, you know?"

Covington grinned. "When was the last time you were around this many black people?"

"Um ... maybe never."

"I understand about being nervous about that," Covington said. "Believe me, I do. Okay, let's grab the bags and head for the parking lot and I'll run interference for you. I already told my Mom where I'd be."

"Do you ever go into white churches?" Wiegand asked.

"Once in a while. No offense, but you got to have a church-full of black people to really bring down the Spirit. If you want to know the truth, I sort of don't understand why white people go to church anyway. I mean, what do they get out of it?"

"You won't find out from me."

A few volunteers were directing traffic out of the parking lot. With a grin at Covington, a white-haired man waved them past the chain-link fence and out on to the street. They headed east toward the expressway. As they coasted into the first stop sign, another ring of refraction in the light swept over them.

"Okay, something is seriously strange here," Covington said. "I saw that one moving, so it's fast but not speed of light or anything. I didn't feel anything, did you?"

"No, but I think it has some effect. I mean, like everybody in the church took a breath at the same time. Did you see anything move, leaves or something?"

"Not that I noticed," Covington said. "It's not radiation or anything electromagnetic. It moves like a shock wave but ..." he was silent for a long moment, then shook his head. "Nah, I got nothin'."

"Same here," Wiegand said. "Could they be blasting, doing some work on the expressway? No, wait a second, we know it's not a shock wave or we'd hear it. Hell."

A few blocks later they went over the expressway bridge. Covington looked down at the road just as two waves flickered past them within a few seconds. Cars were stopped in the middle of the lanes, the drivers standing beside the doors and looking around helplessly. Car horns began to sound.

"I'll take State street," Wiegand said, turning away from the ramp. "Well, it has one physical effect, anyway," he said. "It ties up traffic on the Dan Ryan."

"That narrows it down," Covington laughed. "Only about nine thousand things are known to do that."

The traffic was still Sunday-morning light and State street was mostly empty. There was another wave, and two blocks later, still another. Cars ahead of them pulled to the curb, but Wiegand kept going.

Wiegand drove carefully, his hands nervously tight on the steering wheel. As they passed 59th Street, a series of waves passed through. They saw a pigtailed little black girl stop her scooter on the sidewalk and step off, looking around nervously.

At 47th Street the waves came faster, and faster again at 39th Street. By the time Wiegand pulled into the parking lot at the university and opened the gate with his passcard, the waves were pulsing every ten seconds or so. They parked and got cautiously out. Students stood in staring, silent groups on the lawns between the austere steel and glass buildings.

"Pete," Covington said wonderingly, "I'm seeing both sides of the rings. They're originating from somewhere around here."

"Look at the second floor," Wiegand said tightly. "That's where they're coming from."

"That's our lab."

"Bingo." They ran for the building entrance and burst through the glass doors. The hallway was dim after the outside sunlight, and cool with air conditioning. They dodged past a few dumbstruck students and ran clatteringly up the stairs to the second floor. Wiegand fumbled out the keys to the lab and managed to get the door open.

The lab was full of sunlight from the ceiling-high windows. The Dense Memory Device was a chip the size of a collar button, buried in the middle of a tangle of cables and liquid-nitrogen piping on a bench. Soundless, forceless waves expanded from the chip, twisting the sunlight into ripples. Next to the Device, the jukebox robot twitched its arm to pluck a DVD from the spindle. It whirled, stopped and selected another disk from a rack of hundreds. The robot arm sprung back and mounted the new disk, which whined as it spun up.

The waves were impalpable, but Wiegand and Covington both leaned forward as they approached the bench, as though they were walking against a high wind. Their feet began to lose purchase and they slipped uselessly.

The chip was glowing, the light welling up through the thicket of cables and pipes.

Covington reached for the big red panic switch he had installed. It should have shut off the liquid-nitrogen pump, closed the valves, snapped off all the power. But he never reached it. As Wiegand watched, open-mouthed, the waves seemed to carry away Covington's substance. His outstretched arm grew patchy and transparent. He faded, wavered and was gone.

Wiegand saw with horror his own body fade, and then he was gone too.

The light from the Dense Memory Device dimmed and blinked out. The chip had vanished as well, and the cables were no longer connected to anything. Nitrogen boiled into air and congealed suddenly into clouds. The waves ceased, and placid sunlight poured in from the window undisturbed. The spinning DVD coasted to a halt, and the lab was silent.

Chapter 2

Wiegand gasped. The breath of air he drew in was hot, stinking, and full of bugs. He coughed and retched, and a thick wave of fetid water drenched his head from behind. He tried to sit up but his body was buried in mud. He flapped his arms and legs in uncoordinated panic and managed to get on top of most of the mud, with his face out of the swamp water.

The ground was moving, shaking left and right. Wiegand had never been in an earthquake but pure instinct took over. He lurched up, fell over again as his legs sank in the loose mud, and managed to throw himself up a bank of more solid ground. He clutched coarse grass and pulled himself forward. He was naked.

There was a strangled cry behind him. Wiegand looked back and saw another naked man thrashing in the mud. Wiegand turned on his belly and crawled forward to extend his hand to the other, who grabbed it convulsively. Wiegand's body was slippery with mud and he grabbed the grass as well as he could while he pulled the other up on the bank. When the man was out of the water, both of them sprawled face down and clutched the bucking ground. Their ears were filled with a locomotive roar all around them, further pulverizing any thought.

After a time the shaking stopped and the noise quieted, and a long while after that Wiegand lifted his head to vomit up the water he had swallowed. He rolled over to look around.

Everything was wrong.

The world had only two colors, blue and white. The ground was dark midnight blue, the grass a navy blue except for a white tip at the point of each leaf. There was a blue-trunked tree in front on him with blue leaves like ribbons. Wiegand held his hand in front of him, and his skin was as white as a refrigerator door where it was not smeared with navy-blue mud.

It was not his hand. He made a fist, relaxed it, wiggled the fingers. The hand responded, but the fingers were too short, the thumb too wide, the skin too white and not hairy enough on the back. Not at all his hand.

He held up his other hand, which was just as alien. He endured shock after shock as he examined his genitals, his feet, his belly. It was, really, a body in far better shape than his own couch-potato self, but it was someone else's body he was in.

He rolled on to his back and stared at the sky. The sky was also blue and white. It was a sunny day but there was no sun. Instead, the light came from shining, insubstantial white arches and domes in the blue firmament. The glowing shapes looked to be as distant as stars. There were arches that spanned the horizon, narrower arches that penetrated the others, fragments and traceries of white against the summer-blue sky. He had a sudden memory of a field trip his school had taken to the state capitol building. He had sneaked off to one side to lie on the floor under the Assembly dome, and stared up into the curved roof. This sky was like that.

The total of all the light was enough to illuminate the ground brightly.

The other man had gotten up on his knees. "Jesus," he said, after clearing his throat several times, "I know you're always with me and You will never leave me, and I thank You, Lord, I just thank You for loving me and protecting me. I know You won't ask anything of me I can't handle, and I love You, Jesus, and ... and thank You." His voice trailed off. His breath was raspy and loud.

"Brian?" Wiegand asked. "Is that you?"

The other man was short, wide-shouldered and strongly muscled, not at all like Covington's skinny tall figure. His skin was milky white where it was not smeared with blue mud, and his hair was navy blue. As he turned, Wiegand could see that his hair grew down the back of his neck and became a ruff along his spine.

"Pete?" the other said.

"Yeah, it's me." They both stood and looked at each other.

"You're not in your right body," Covington said.

"Yeah, you neither. Also we're on an alien planet, or something," Wiegand said.

"Sure as hell." They spent a few silent minutes, looking at the swampy two-color landscape and their own bodies. The trees were short and withy, with blue ribbon leaves brushing the blue ground, surrounded by spiky grass twinkling with white tips.

The air was bright and hazy and still stank terribly of unidentifiable chemicals and swamp rot.

Wiegand discovered he had the same ruff of blue hair along his own spine. He realized that he had no bellybutton, and neither did Covington.

"Well, what happened?" Wiegand said finally.

"The Dense Memory Device went all weird-ball on us, and then we woke up naked in somebody else's body in red mud," Covington said. "That's all I know."

"Red mud? Is that what you see? Everything looks blue and white to me."

"To me everything is dark red and white, with little flashes of yellow on some of the edges," Covington said.

"Peach-a-reeno," Wiegand mumbled. "You suppose we're inside a video game, like *Tron*?"

"Or we just woke up from a video game, like *Matrix*," Covington said. After a few deep breaths, he grinned, showing white teeth behind blue lips. "Personally, I think we touched the magic eight-ball and were transported to Barsoom or someplace, where we will meet alien princesses who will fall in love with us. After we kill big monsters, I mean."

Wiegand held up a hand that did not seem to be his, with blue dirt under the fingernails, and started ticking off ideas. "One, we're plain crazy — no, the hell with that, this doesn't feel like crazy. Two, there were drugs in the donuts at your church. Three, we're on Talos IV and the Talosians are messing with our minds. Um, maybe the Dense Memory Device threw us into an alternate reality or the Purple Brain Dimension or something. Five or six or whatever I'm on, there was some powerful wizard, Christopher

Lee or somebody, who mixed up a magic potion and drew us here to Magicland. How'm I doing?"

"No, it can't be that last one," Covington said.

"Why not?"

"Because that would be a sucky movie and I don't want to be in that movie."

"An important point!" Wiegand announced cheerfully. "Okay, no wizards."

"Pete, no joke, this *can't* be real," Covington said. "I mean, look at us, we're *Star Trek* aliens."

"What do you mean?"

"I mean aliens who just happen to look exactly like human character actors except for having funny noses, which is very convenient for the casting department and keeps the show on budget. This is definitely not my body, but any decent makeup man could tint my skin white and paste the red hair on my spine in half an hour. That doesn't happen in real life."

"Well, but, you know, here we are."

"I know why *Star Trek* does aliens that way — because it's cheap. I can't conceive that Mother Nature would do it. There's just no way in hell that aliens can wind up looking exactly like human beings. There are just too many variables."

"Even human beings without bellybuttons," Wiegand said.

"Sumbitch!" Covington said. "I didn't notice. I feel like I'm in ... I don't know, a sausage casing or something. Not a body that belongs to me."

"Me, too," Wiegand said. "You know what? I think we were just created there in that mud. I mean, as opposed to somebody throwing us into it or something. From the smell, I'd say there are enough

19

chemicals in that slime to build a body or almost anything."

"Jesus, help me now," Covington said in a low voice.

"Hey, it could be the alien scientists invented a brain-switching machine, and they're walking around on Earth in our bodies right now stealing atomic secrets. Man, I watch too much TV," Wiegand said. "I'll tell you what. Let's say *you* are on the alien planet Zoomabar with monsters and princesses, but *I* have been sucked into a video game with very high resolution graphics, stinky smell-o-vision and apparently only 4-bit color. That's my story and I'm stickin' to it."

Covington looked at him. His mouth worked but he could not get a word out.

Wiegand paused for a long moment, then said in a low voice, "God, Brian, I'm sorry. I'm *so* full of crap. I'm sorry. I'm sorry, I'm just talking too much."

Covington began to cry and Wiegand followed a moment later, both of them crumpling to the ground and hugging themselves. They sobbed helplessly and loudly for minutes, rolling back and forth. After a while their wailing quieted and they lay spent for a moment, until they both had to begin slapping at insects.

"All right," Covington said presently, sitting up. "I needed that. Jesus, thank You for helping me get my head straight. But we've got to get out of this swamp. I'm getting eaten alive."

Wiegand had recovered himself also. "Yeah, if this is a video game it's entirely too damn realistic, at least about the bugs. You notice the bugs are all the same color, too?"

"And so are the bug bites." Covington got painfully to his feet and looked around. "I think the only solid ground is that way," he said, pointing in the featureless mist. "I don't want to get back in that water, it looks nasty."

"Smells, too," Wiegand said, standing up. "Man, I just know we're about to find out how you earn points in this video game, and I know I'm going to hate it."

"We're not going to go fast," Covington said. "This ground is all churned up. There isn't a flat place to walk anywhere."

"What busted up all this ground?"

"Hello? Earthquake?"

"Oh, yeah, that," Wiegand said. "You think maybe we caused the earthquake? By appearing here, I mean?"

They stepped clumsily through the muddy upheaval while Covington considered. "No," he said finally. "Something released a hell of a lot of energy here, a lot more than we could possibly account for. Look at all the trees that are knocked over. I suppose maybe it could happen that we appeared here *because* there was so much energy in play. I'm just guessing. I don't know anything."

"Hey, check it out!" Wiegand said. "A road."

They stumbled out on what was undoubtedly a paved road, although the pavement was buckled into tilted plates. It was narrow, more like a country lane than a highway, and it was built on a bed of gravel a couple of inches higher than the soggy ground. It stretched in both directions. To Wiegand's eyes, the gravel was white, the paving material blue-black.

"There's a sign," Covington said, pointing to a placard mounted on a stick. It appeared white with blue printing to Wiegand, with a strange symbol and unreadable writing. "At least we know some of the traffic goes that way."

"I was expecting it to be in English," Wiegand muttered. They stepped out on the pitched chunks of road, which were slimy with blue mud, and headed in the direction of the sign.

"What the hell? Why would it be in English?"

"On the planet Zoomabar they always speak English. They learned it by studying the Earth with powerful telescopes."

Covington was silent long enough to draw a couple of deep breaths. "Pete?" he said dangerously.

"Yeah?"

"Shut up, okay? It's been a difficult day already."

"Sorry, Brian," Wiegand said. "Sorry, sorry."

The mist was still thick even though the day was growing lighter. As they walked, Wiegand realized that not all of the light was coming from the structures in the sky. The tips of the blades of grass around them were not just white, they were glowing a little, and the light from the ground added to the illumination. They still could not see far ahead.

The road curved to the right, and Covington pointed above the mist. "Mountains," he said. "Pretty far off, I think. Looks like snow on the tops."

Wiegand peered, then said, "I don't think it's snow. I think the mountain tops are glowing, like the grass here."

"The grass glows? Sure enough?" Covington stepped off the road and lay on his stomach on the grass. He cupped his hands around his face to provide some darkness and examined the grass. "It is glowing," he said, getting up.

"We'll just add that to the weirdness list," Wiegand said sourly.

"Get ready to write a lot more on the weirdness list," Covington said. "We're coming into town." The road curved again and they could see a village of wooden shacks ahead of them, past another roadside sign which presumably said something about "Welcome to Our Hamlet."

The village had suffered cruelly in the earthquake. A few of the white wooden buildings had survived, but many more were sprawled across the blue ground. Blue smoke rose from white-flamed fires. Rescue parties were lifting the fallen walls to look for survivors.

All of the people were porcelain-white with blue hair and features, to Wiegand's eyes. All had the ruffs of blue hair extending to their shoulders and down their spines. Both men and women wore broad flat hats. The men generally wore pullover shirts with v-necks in front and back, presumably to accommodate their back hair. They had shorts and boots. There were women in the same pullover shirts with loose full-length trousers gathered at the ankles. A few small children stood to one side, awed and anxious.

A party of men and women were hoisting the wooden wall of a fallen house off the ground when Wiegand and Covington walked up. It had tipped over in one piece. "Here, we can help," Wiegand said, and a couple of the men stared at them but grunted acknowledgment in a language they could not understand.

They took places along the fallen wall to lift it. Working together, they pushed the wall up and tipped it to fall over the other way. There was an old man on the ground who had been under the wall. His face was messy with blue blood but he was alive and conscious. Two of the women helped him up and walked him away to a collection of tables that had been dragged together to make a first-aid station.

Three of the men tried to talk to Covington and Wiegand, but they understood nothing. After a few sentences, the others stopped trying.

"They're staring at us," Wiegand said.

"Yeah. Oh, you know why? It's because we don't have any pants on."

"Oh, crap," Wiegand said. "I didn't even think of that. First I forgot about an earthquake, and now I forgot about pants. You know, my brain didn't work all that well even back in my real body."

"I didn't think of it either," Covington said. "I feel like I'm wearing a trick-or-treat costume anyway. It doesn't feel like *me* who's naked."

Actually, the people in the work party stared at the Earthmen's heads and seemed more disturbed by their lack of hats than pants. As they walked wearily to the next fallen building, several of them searched the rubble for clothes. They finally tied ragged kerchiefs on the heads of Covington and Wiegand, and only afterward brought them shorts and boots.

The shorts were loose but had belts that could be tightened.

The party flipped another fallen wooden wall and uncovered the body of a woman, crushed, broken and dead. The women and two of the men in the party gasped and cried. Two others brusquely picked up the body and carried it to a morgue that had been set up on a patch of ground nearby. They trudged on.

The ground around each of the tumbled houses was full of the litter of living: tin cans, bottles (made of an opaque blue glass, apparently), clothes, furniture. They picked out unbroken cans of food and drink and piled them together. One house had a supply of bandages and medicines, another a tarpaulin they salvaged to be used as a tent.

"Pete," Covington said, "all these houses are exactly the same." They peered through the open kitchen door of a house that had not fallen but was leaning outrageously. The shelves along the walls were empty, and the floor was thick with cans and broken bottles. They did not go in.

"I noticed that," Wiegand said. "I think it's some kind of company town or something else that was built all at once. They're all really small and cheap, too."

"I think the whole town only had a couple hundred people," Covington said, "and it looks like twenty or thirty dead at least. God, take care of them, please."

"Uh, oh. There's a live kid in this one. Do we have any rope?"

Wiegand tried to pantomime the idea of "rope" and finally got it across to one of the men, who ran down the muddy street and borrowed a coil of rope from another party.

"Okay," Wiegand said to the others, ignoring the difficulty that they could not understand him. "Brian, you get on the one side and prop up that wall, but stand on the corner so you can jump out of the way if it falls. You there, you take the other corner. You two, let's put the rope through the windows like this ... okay, now you take one end and you grab on for dear life. The idea is to not let the wall fall down on me, okay? Okay!"

They pulled on the rope, and Covington and the other man pushed against the leaning wall on the other side. Wiegand stepped in gingerly, moving anxiously but quickly. He crossed the ruined kitchen floor, stepping lightly, snatched up a live but unconscious toddler from under a pile of furniture, and carefully returned. When he reached the door, he walked out jauntily and handed the child to one of the women, who carried it away.

"Now we're big friends, right?" he said to one and all, and in fact the others smiled and patted him on the back. He smacked his chest in the time-honored gesture and said "Pete Wiegand!" Then he pointed to the nearest man, a burly short fellow with the blue hair on his head trimmed close. (No one seemed to trim the back and spine hair.)

That man thumped his own chest, grinned and said "Dogat Arrhem."

The man next to him repeated the gesture and announced himself as "Dogat Hell Esmer." Next to him was a rather pretty young woman who named herself "Dogat Sinsin." The others also had names beginning with "Dogat."

Covington introduced himself and tried to shake hands, but that didn't seem to be the custom. The group started down a lane between piles of debris, which had been a street. "So is 'Dogat' a family name, or a title like 'Mister'?" Wiegand asked.

"Or it means 'My name is'," Covington said. "Or it's a rank like 'Corporal' and they're all corporals in the local Civil Defense Corps. We don't know anything."

Wiegand pointed to himself and said "Dogat Pete!" The others frowned and shook their heads -- at least that gesture was the same. "Well," he said. "Whatever 'Dogat' is, I don't get to be one."

The work was heartbreaking and hard. They found and stacked more dead bodies, but did not find any more injured. They put out scattered fires by carrying water from the swamp (never far away from any place in the town) and searched for usable food, drink and bedding.

"Look over there," Covington said. "A couple of big buildings."

"Looks like a factory," Wiegand said. "I thought this looked like a company town. Probably everybody in town works there or is married to somebody who does."

"The building over that way looks like a church, or some kind of meeting hall," Covington said. "Lotta people gathered around it."

"Or it's just a big building that's still standing," Wiegand said.

The work party, led by Dogat Arrhem, worked their way over to the meeting hall, and clearly the rest of the town was headed there as well. The people there had collected doors and other flat boards to make beds, and were moving the injured inside to make a hospital. Others had built rough tables and started cooking fires. Wiegand and Covington were both dragging blankets loaded up with cans and bottles. They gratefully accepted tin pans of stew and bottles of drink from the people working at their rough kitchen and sat on the ground in a circle with the others from their group. They ate with their fingers, and the others called out weary greetings and questions to passersby.

The Earthmen, like any foreigners at dinner, tried a few exaggerated facial expressions and gestures to indicate "Good food!," then gave up and talked to each other. "How's yours?" Covington asked.

"Not bad, considering I'm hungry enough to eat mud," Wiegand said. "Tastes kind of like ... I don't know, oatmeal with apples. The drink could be tea, almost."

"Oh, yeah? To me, the stew tastes sort of like chili with pieces of candy in it. The drink is just water."

"You still seeing everything as red?"

"Red and white, yeah."

"To me," Wiegand said, "everything and everybody still looks blue and white."

"You know what?" Covington said. "I don't think anything here is really any color we've ever seen, and I don't think we've ever tasted any food like this, and probably we don't smell things the same -- no, don't tell me about what you smell. I think our brains are going crazy trying to interpret our senses."

"I'll buy it," Wiegand said, yawning. "You remember that experiment they did where they made these guys wear upside-down glasses, and they bumped around for a couple of weeks until they woke up one morning and suddenly they could see right-side up? Then when they took off the glasses, everything looked upside down again until they got their brains adjusted back."

"That could happen to us, our brains could adjust themselves," Covington said. "Oh, God, I wonder how long we're going to be here?"

"I don't think we're going anywhere," Wiegand said. He gave Covington an unconvincing grin and said, "I'll be glad to get my colors back. Some of these women would look pretty good if they weren't blue. I can live with the hair down the back."

"Well, there you are," Covington said. "We're in alien bodies, our eyes are screwed up, our noses don't work right, but the sex hormones are cookin' right along."

When the meal was over, everyone gathered by the door of the hall. A team of men went inside and brought out two bulky wooden structures. They were long troughs mounted on wooden legs that held them tilted at an angle, about chin-high at one end down to knee-high at the other. The men went back inside to bring out four decorated wooden barrels, two filled with water.

At the same time, another group brought out a wooden platform and set it on the ground. The speaker who stepped up on it was an old man wearing a more elaborate hat than the others. "Okay, it's a church," Covington said. "I can tell a preacher when I see one."

"How about that? Even here in Never-Never Land you managed to hook up with the holy rollers."

"Hush."

The preacher spoke for a few minutes, obviously giving a message of comfort and hope that his audience seemed to like. Then they all stood and everyone except the two Earthmen sang a hymn.

The crowd sorted themselves into two queues, the men lined up at one wooden trough and the women at the other. In batches of about twenty, they moved to stand on both sides of the trough and put one hand inside. Two men lifted a barrel of water at the high end and poured it slowly down the trough into an empty barrel at the low end. When the upper barrel was empty, the people moved away without drying their wet hands and the process repeated.

"I kind of like that!" Covington said, watching this process. "That's a good ceremony. We're all in the river of life together, we go with the flow, our sins get washed away ... that kind of works for me. We should go get in line."

"We're outsiders," Wiegand said. "We may not be invited."

"They shared their food, didn't they? Anyway, the only way to find out is to try it."

"They might get mad if we horn in."

"They might get mad if we don't get our hands wet. They might be crazy religious fanatics who have sworn to kill the dry-hand heretics. Pete, we don't know *anything*, but they've been okay to us so far and besides, you rescued one of their kids. Come on, let's go see what they say."

They fell in at the end of the men's line and became part of the last batch. The ritual was accompanied by speaking a phrase which of course they didn't know, but no one seemed very put off by that. They stood with the others, got their hands wet and then returned to their group. The preacher stood up to say a few more words, there was a round of call-and-response answers from the crowd and the ceremony was over. However, the preacher also pointed up the road that led into the town and added some remarks, and everyone cheered.

There was a party of "horse" carts coming up the road, presumably called to help from some other town. The men driving the carts looked no different from the town men, but the draft animals pulling the wooden wagons made Covington and Wiegand stare in amazement.

"I think the special-effects budget just went up," Wiegand said. "The people may be Star Trek aliens but those critters are either really good CGI or ..."

"Those animals," Covington said, "did not evolve on the same planet as humans. They just didn't. If they're natives, then the people came here from someplace else, or the other way around."

The "horses" had shaggy hides (dark blue, to Wiegand's eyes), six legs and round heads with four small stupid eyes equally spaced around the circumference. Their bones, at least the larger ones, were on the outside of their bodies. Each leg had a white thighbone, a separate knee and a shin bone clutched to the outside of the leg by fleshy knobs. The muscles were working under the blue pelts, but the articulation was exterior.

"That one had a broken leg bone," Wiegand said, pointing. "You can see where somebody patched up that bone."

"Look at the one on the third wagon," Covington said. "I guess the bone was ruined, because I think Farmer Jones carved a replacement bone out of wood. The knob-things are holding the wooden bone just like the others."

The procession pulled up by the church, with many greetings all around, and stretcher parties began taking the injured patients out of the church building and loading them into the carts.

Dogat Arrhem tapped both Earthmen on the shoulders, and motioned for them to join the caravan of carts. Some of the casualties stayed in the church building, and it didn't take long to load up the wagons with the rest. Within half an hour, the carts were back on the road, going away from the town and swamp. About thirty of the townspeople walked alongside and between the carts, talking to and tending the injured patients. Covington and Wiegand walked with them.

They were no more than a mile out of town when Covington grabbed Wiegand and pointed up in the sky. There was some kind of a flying ship high above them, coming lower. It was shaped like a hamburger bun, a wide cylinder with a domed top, and had no wings or jets. It was large, bigger than a house, and moved silently across the sky. It sailed above them and continued in the same direction they were going, gliding easily a few hundred feet in the air.

"Spaceships," Wiegand said. "Horse carts pulled by alien horses and now anti-gravity spaceships. I did *not* need that."

"I suppose ships like that either brought the horses or brought the people here. Maybe we can get a ride back to Earth."

"Or maybe they brought us here in the first place. My weird-o-meter just went into the red. You know what?" Wiegand said. "I really hate this. I hate this whole planet. If it is a planet."

"Amen to that," Covington said. They walked on.

Chapter 3

The "horses" plodded along at a good pace, with the people keeping up wearily on foot. Dogat Arrhem was in the party, walking alongside a wagon whose four injured passengers included a woman with a broken leg, crudely splinted with boards tied on with rags. He held her hand and talked to her.

Covington walked alongside them, and tried to offer sympathy. "Arrhem," he said.

"Dogat Arrhem," the other corrected him absently.

"Dogat Arrhem," Covington said. He pointed to the woman, then patted the man on his back. Dogat Arrhem nodded his thanks, and the woman said something as well.

There was a noise on the road behind them, and the drivers pulled all the wagons to one side. The rest of the crowd stepped off the road, and the Earthmen watched in amazement as a motor truck pulled up and passed them. It had six wheels and a freight bed loaded with sealed blue barrels. The driver was human and waved politely to them, but did not offer to let anyone ride as he continued on. When the truck had passed, the rest of the party returned to the road.

"Damn!" Wiegand said. "If they've got trucks like that, why are we walking with animal carts?" He pointed at the receding truck and spread his hands, looking at Dogat Arrhem.

They had no language in common, but Dogat Arrhem's response in gestures and facial expressions could not have been clearer. He "said" two things. First, that he was angry about it also, and second, "But the hell with it, what are you gonna do?"

They walked for an hour or so, and it began to get dark. There was no sunset. Instead, the airy arches, streamers and domes began to dim, and the sky between them settled into a darker evening blue. The party pulled off the road into a meadow of blue grass. They arranged blankets, rags and spare clothing over the casualties to keep them warm, and what items of clothing that were left over were distributed to the walkers. Covington and Wiegand each received a shirt, which they put on gratefully.

Apparently those who were not in the wagons were going to simply sleep on the grass or under the wagons. It was cooler, but not really cold, and the insects were not as bad as in the swamp. "I suppose there's some reason not to travel at night," Wiegand said. "If it was me, I'd get these people to a doctor faster, assuming that's what we're doing."

"Yeah," Covington said. "Look, I'm going to go over there and pray for a while."

"Do you want me to go with you?"

"No, me and God need some one-on-one time, or at least I need it. You get some sleep if you can."

"Thanks," Wiegand said. The sky did not become entirely dark, but the white arches faded to ghostly shells dripping faint light, precessing slowly across the sky. The glowing tops of the distant mountains were still visible from the direction they had come. He lay back on the grass and looked up, and realized that the pattern in the sky had changed since he was "born" that morning. There were no stars, no moon, nothing that was familiar in the sky except some cumulus clouds that looked exactly like Earth clouds. There was a thin white haze visible behind the dark sky, like seeing the Milky Way.

Everyone else was already asleep, both the casualties and the townsfolk with them. Quite a few of them were snoring already. They did not post guards, did not have anyone awake to take care of the patients.

Wiegand was dead tired, too tired and stressed to sleep. He watched the show in the sky. The big arches overhead remained dim, but there were smaller arches and lines and a few complete circles visible near the horizon, and they brightened and dimmed again irregularly.

Covington came back, lay down and was snoring almost immediately.

Wiegand lay with his mind racing, overwhelmed with loneliness and shock. He dozed a little but never really slept, and was awake when light began to fill up an arch overhead and the daylight returned.

Everyone awoke, and they passed out water and slabs of what tasted like cold meat (Wiegand hoped it was meat) for breakfast, anxious to get going again. In a few minutes, the carts were creaking along the road.

"Brian," Wiegand said, "it's hard to tell without a clock and everything screwy anyway, but I think that 'night' was only a couple of hours long."

"For real?" Covington considered it. "Yeah, could be. I was out like a log, but I sort of feel like I didn't sleep very long. But you know, I'm tired from walking but I'm not sleepy. Nobody else looks real sleepy either."

"I am, because I didn't sleep, but yeah, everybody else zonked right out. I don't know, maybe the night just seemed short."

After another hour of walking, the wild lands gave way to farm fields. "You have any idea what they're growing?" Wiegand asked.

"I'm a city boy," Covington said. "I can pick out corn and marijuana. After that, I'm not much on identifying crops. But hell, we wouldn't expect these to be Earth plants."

"Yeah." The crops were bushy plants, blue like everything else, a foot high and planted in neat rows. The fields were separated by windrows of tall trees, and there were fairly ordinary-looking farmhouses here and there. They passed one fenced-in field with animals grazing.

"Hey, those must be the local equivalent of cows or something," Wiegand said. "They don't look like any Earth animal but, you know, they could have been."

"Sort of like small hippos with lots of curly hair," Covington said. "I bet they shear them like sheep. But yeah, those look like they could evolve on the same planet with humans. Not like the horse-things."

"Shows you how beat down we are. I'm pathetically grateful to see something that's slightly less weird than everything else."

"I know what you mean, Pete," Covington said.

The road widened, and they were passed by several other carts drawn by the alien horses, driven apparently by farmers taking produce into the city. They all had a word of sympathy for the Dogat casualties, and paused for a little conversation before continuing. There were also a few motor trucks. The drivers waved and seemed friendly but did not offer rides as they breezed past. Another spaceship descended and drifted silently over them, evoking no interest at all from anyone except the Earthmen.

The road descended into a shallow valley, and there was a city spread out before them. In Illinois, it would have been a minor map dot, but it was far larger than the other village. They could see a "downtown" of taller buildings in the center, perhaps four stories high, and a broad expanse of streets with houses and other buildings. A river curled around it.

The buildings were more or less ordinary, mostly built of wood, with rectangular walls and peaked roofs. Most were white, but many of them were presumably painted in various colors which Wiegand saw only as shades of blue. There were a few taller buildings, some of them topped with domes or steeples that might have indicated churches, and a section of warehouses near a flat area on the periphery that immediately suggested a small-town airport.

In fact, the "airport" was a spaceport, because several of the hamburger-bun spaceships were parked there. Wiegand pointed it out to Covington.

"A port city!" Covington said. "You know what we can find there?"

"Bars and whores? Passage to Earth? Old sailors with tall stories?"

"Jobs."

"I was kind of hoping we'd be magically transported back home the same way we got here," Wiegand said. "At least, before we had to get jobs or anything mundane."

Covington's grin fell. "Yeah, I want to get home too. But, Pete, I don't think we should expect that. I don't think we should expect anything, really."

"Except death and taxes, and don't you just know this will turn out to be the kind of Purple Brain Dimension where they have taxes? Actually, take a look at that town. Does it strike you that it looks like a housing development too? I mean all the buildings are pretty much in the same style and I kind of think they're all the same age, fairly new."

"Now that you mention it, yeah. Also the earthquake doesn't seem to have reached here, or at least it didn't do any damage I can see."

"True." The road was joined by other roads now and there was a thicker traffic of people on foot, animal carts and freight trucks. There was also the sound of a car horn, a loud and obnoxious one, and the crowd pulled to the sides of the road as a private car sped through.

There was a driver and one passenger. They were not human. Covington and Wiegand had a glimpse of two torsos with wide headless shoulders, covered in plush blue fur. The blue-and-white car breezed past at high speed and was gone in moments. "Cortay!" Dogat Arrhem said with disgust.

"Aliens driving cars," Covington said to Wiegand. "I suppose we should have known they'd have aliens, after seeing the horses. I guess they're named 'Cortays.'"

"Unless 'Cortay' means 'jerk,'" Wiegand said.

"Or possibly all Cortays are jerks and act like that."

The town was directly surrounded by farm fields, and there was no wall or even a fence marking the perimeter. They plodded past the outer row of houses and were on a commercial street heading toward the center. The streets were wide and paved, very dusty and messy with blue mud, and smelled of what was presumably excrement from the "horses". Pedestrians and horse carts kept to the sides, leaving the center mostly open for trucks and presumably passenger cars, although there did not seem to be any others around.

The buildings here had stores at the street level, with apartments on the second floor above them, decorated with hand-painted advertising. The shopkeepers often stood outside and hailed the passers-by to try vegetables, hats, kitchenware, rolls of cloth, clocks, books or liquor. Wiegand pointed to an open-air bar — just a few tables and chairs in an empty lot, with two vendors offering bottles from carts parked at the back. A couple of friendly drunks waved to them. Covington nodded. "Yeah, we get those in my neighborhood sometimes."

All of the wagons carrying the injured turned up one street, probably heading for the local hospital, but Dogat Arrhem kept straight with the two outsiders following. He led them to another storefront, also festooned with signs and with a symbol of two wavy parallel lines over the door.

"They had that river thing painted on the church yesterday," Wiegand said.

"I know what this is," Covington said. "It's a church rescue mission. It just has that look."

"What does that mean?"

"It means we're on Skid Row. We'll get some soup as long as we sing some hymns, and we get to meet the neighborhood winos. The ones who don't have a buck for Mad Dog, I mean."

"Well, I could use some soup. For that matter, I'd like a bottle of Mad Dog."

Dogat Arrhem had some conversation with a round-faced young man in front of this establishment. This fellow, who wore a cap with a long brim, beamed at them all, pointed to himself and introduced himself as "Sad For Elkanicut."

Covington pointed to himself and said, "Brian Covington."

"Sad For Brian Covington," Sad For Elkanicut said, smiling even wider and mangling the pronunciation considerably. Pete Wiegand went through the same ritual and also had "Sad For" added to his name.

On a hunch, Wiegand turned to Arrhem and tried the name "Sad For Dogat Arrhem" to address him. Arrhem drew back, offended, and said "Dogat Arrhem."

"Okay, he's a 'Dogat' and we are 'Sad For's,'" Covington said. "I hope it's more like being a member of the Presbyterians, rather than, you know, being a member of the Insane Vice Lords."

"I'd put Reverend Slick, here, as more the Presbyterian type," Wiegand said. He made a questioning face to Elkanicut and asked "Sad For?"

"Sad For!" Elkanicut exclaimed, still with his welcome-the-unfortunate-clients smile. He waved to indicate the town around them.

"'Sad For' is the *town*?" Covington said in English. "The *town* is part of our name?"

Elkanicut could not have understood any of this speech but waved again and said a few proud words about Sad For. He opened the door and gestured them into his building.

"Well, we have a recognized place in this society now," Covington said as they went in.

"What's that?"

"We're homeless crazy guys on Skid Row."

Chapter 4

The main room inside was a meeting hall with wooden folding chairs and a slanted water trough with buckets, like that in the Dogat church. There was a river symbol worked in polished wood mounted on the wall, and a few floor lamps with flat, white, shining heads shaped like the spades from a deck of cards.

Two stern, no-nonsense old women in close-fitting hats took charge of them and led them away to a concrete shower room, indicating that they would wash themselves without any back chat. Covington and Wiegand were sweaty and grimy and desperate for a shower even in cold water. They complied readily, tossing their soiled clothing out to the women. There were bars of gritty soap and they washed luxuriantly, then dried themselves on scratchy towels.

They marched out naked and the women gave them hats first, followed by shorts and too-large pullover shirts. The hats were more or less sombreros, with wide upturned brims and tall peaks. "Oh, we're stylin' now," Wiegand said.

"Considering this is a church mission," Covington said, "I'm willing to bet these hats were the height of style maybe fifteen or twenty years ago, and finally Grandma made Grampa give them up for the poor. Did you see anybody outside wearing these?"

"No, but I wasn't thinking about it." He did an ironic little fashion-runway walk with the hat. The women favored him with a sour look and led him over to a bin of dusty shoes to find a pair that fit better than what he had.

"I think we might just as well carry signboards that say 'Wino!'," Covington said gloomily. "Everybody that sees us is going to know we got these clothes at the rescue mission."

When they were dressed, they were led back into the main hall, where a few other men waited. Most of them had an untidy look that marked them as the regular clientele. They all seemed to know each other and were slyly joking and greeting each other by name. Many of them wore the sombreros. Also, Wiegand noted, a number of them mixed an unwashed smell with an odor something like curry powder and cinnamon, which certainly suggested the local equivalent of "alcoholic".

There was also a young man, neater and more fit than the others, who did not seem to be part of the crowd. He had hair that was perhaps really blonde but looked white to Wiegand, and was wearing worn but neat coveralls that might have been a uniform. He was in good spirits and trying to talk to the others, although it was obvious he did not speak the local language either.

The regulars knew the routine and sat down quickly when Sad For Elkanicut came in and walked to a lectern. He delivered a genial and pleasantly short talk, clearly a sermon, and afterward clapped a number of the men on the shoulder (carefully but unobtrusively choosing a clean spot on their coats to touch). He waited while the two old women returned, one carrying a musical instrument like a cello. Everyone sang a hymn which the three foreigners couldn't follow, then lined up at the "river" trough to get their hands wet together while two volunteers lifted and poured the water barrel.

The winos knew what to do next. They quickly folded the unused chairs and opened up folding tables. In a few moments they had set up the tables, laid out sporks (Wiegand wondered if everyone used them, or just Skid Row missions or just poor people?) and bowls, and poured water in glasses.

Elkanicut and the women sat together while two regulars went into the kitchen and returned with a big pot of stew which they ladled into the bowls, and distributed chunks of dark blue bread. Elkanicut said a quick grace over the meal and everyone dug in. The food was good although Wiegand could not have described the taste.

The winos may have been dirty and smelly but they were friendly enough. As they ate, they cheerfully taught the foreigners the words for "bowl" and "spork" and everything else on the table and in the room. They also grinned as they taught the newcomers a word for the stew, then retreated when one of the women gave them a look that would curdle new milk, and taught them a different word for it. Like good schoolboys, all three outsiders solemnly repeated each term and pretty soon had a vocabulary of perhaps thirty words.

At the end of the meal, Covington and Wiegand were assigned to wash dishes in the kitchen, while the others swept and folded the tables. "At least we landed on a planet with running water," Covington said. "Also flush toilets, thank you Jesus!"

"And electricity," Wiegand added.

"Not sure about that. Did you notice that those standing lamps aren't plugged in to anything? And I don't see any place you could put a battery, either."

"Gas lamps, maybe? Or like firefly light, some kind of chemicals?"

"Hard to say, but the top is just a solid piece of flat metal."

"You know, there's a hinge under the top part," Wiegand said. "You fill up the wash tub for a moment. I'm going to go look." He stepped over to floor lamp that lit the kitchen, examined the hinge, then let the top hang down. The light dimmed and died.

He reset the top to point up again, and it began to glow. He tried this twice more.

Meanwhile, Covington had found a can of white dish soap powder. He sprinkled some into the water and it foamed up in a perfectly ordinary way. "Check this out," he said, pointing to the illustrated, two-color label of the can. "Here's Mrs. Cheerful Housewife who uses this product to make her life delirious. Also, she's a babe. I bet the symbols inside the big circle here are the price, now that I think about it. We should look and see if these symbols appear anyplace else where you would expect to see numbers."

"Just like home," Wiegand said. "You wash and I'll rinse."

There was a rag hanging from the faucet and Covington started washing the bowls. When he got to a spork, he hesitated and stared at it, waving it in his hand. "Pete," he said, "go turn out that light again for a moment, will you?"

Wiegand pulled the metal top of the lamp down on its hinge, and it faded out. Covington held the spork upright. A faint light flickered around the tines. "Watch this," he said. He tilted the spork to the left and the tines grew dark. When he brought it back upright, the glow returned.

45

"The grass outside," Wiegand said. "There was a little white light at the pointed tip."

"And the mountains were glowing, but only at the top," Covington said. "So I guess the rule is that any pointed object glows at least a little when it's facing up, but not when it's facing down or to the side. The lamp must be made of some substance that lights up particularly well. You can turn it back on. Hey, touch the bulb part. Is it warm?"

"No, it isn't," Wiegand said, feeling the metal.

One of the women looked into the kitchen to see what was going on. Covington smiled and held up his rag and the spork and attempted to look like a busy dish washer. She withdrew.

"I guess I missed that day in physics class," Wiegand said, getting back to rinsing and stacking the dishes.

"I didn't," Covington said grimly. "Hell no, I didn't. *Nothing* in the world acts that way. This can't happen."

"Except it is."

"New laws of physics and ordinary grocery-store dish soap," Covington said. "Where are we? Where the *hell* are we?"

The two women had left by the time they finished, along with most of the regular winos. The blonde young man was drying the "river" trough with clean white linen that clearly was not used on ordinary surfaces. Under Sad For Elkanicut's watchful eye, he folded the cloth when he was done and replaced it in a locker. Two other men, much older and obviously regulars, swept the floor.

It was growing dark again. Elkanicut brought them into a little dorm room at the end of a hallway. There were saggy bunk beds with thin mattresses, and he gave them ragged blankets. He waved goodbye to them and let himself out, apparently confident of their good behavior.

The two winos bowed politely and mumbled a few words to the others, then picked bunks, took off their hats for the first time and were asleep in minutes.

Covington named himself to the young foreign man with the same point-at-the-chest gesture as before, but did not add "Sad For" to his name. He identified Wiegand the same way. The fellow grinned and named himself as "Vallow," also without adding "Sad For".

In a few minutes of halting conversation, they were friends facing the world together. It quickly became obvious that Vallow was not an alcoholic. He was as foreign to the town of Sad For as Covington and Wiegand, and did not seem to have been in the rescue mission for long. They shared what few words of the local language they had, grinning and pointing, and since the kitchen was still open, Covington went back for three glasses of water and they had a fine half-hour of companionable drinking.

It was now full dark, and all three were yawning heavily. They retired to their bunks, and Wiegand fell asleep watching the slow-changing show in the sky through one high window.

In the morning, three other women roused them out of bed and prepared a kind of porridge, which they ate in the main hall in the company of a dozen winos off the street, some of whom had also been there the evening before. After breakfast, Covington and Wiegand washed dishes again while the others folded the tables, swept, brought out all of the folding chairs and opened the spade-shaped lamps. After an hour, a much larger congregation began filtering in. They were mostly dissipated men, with a few worn-looking women and a couple of children. The hall filled up. The Earthmen finished their work and were led in to sit with the others. Vallow came to sit with them.

"I'm guessing it's the local equivalent of Sunday," Covington said. "I mean, they're having a morning service and it looks like a crowd."

"I suppose so," Wiegand said. "Looks like these new women are back with the cello thingie. You must be right at home."

"With a *cello*? What's wrong with this picture? Anyway, the only time I was in a rescue mission," Covington said primly, "I was a volunteer from our church."

"Then I'm one-up on you," Wiegand said. "I had a couple of friends from college who were going through a starving-hippie phase in, actually, Cleveland. They wanted to be Beatnik poets, except neither of them had any talent and besides, they were way out of position, being in Ohio instead of California. Anyway, I went to the local bum-relief with them a couple of times."

"Shh. It's starting." Another preacher came in, an older man wearing a hat of complicated folded creases. He led a formalized call-and-response, the women played the cello, the congregation sang without hymnbooks. The priest followed that with a fairly long sermon, then more hymns.

They set up the river trough and everyone lined up to stick their hands in. Women and children used the same trough, but not at the same time as men. The path back from the trough led past a collection basket watched by one of the women. Most of the other people chipped in a coin or two.

After the service there was a lunch of bread and soup, then more dish washing for Covington and Wiegand and cleaning for the others. Finally all of the visitors had left the building and Sad For Elkanicut arrived. With much arm-waving, he managed to convey that the three foreigners could leave and come back later, so they went out for a walk.

"If this is Sunday, then the stores are run by the local equivalent of Jews or Arabs or Koreans or somebody," Covington observed as they stood on the sidewalk. "Doesn't look like anybody's closed."

"Unless they don't have the thing about not working on Sunday," Wiegand said. "Hey, is that guy selling clocks?"

They went to look. The shopkeeper regarded their sombreros dubiously but allowed them to look at his wares as long as they didn't touch any. The clocks were mechanical, with spring knobs in the back and half-circle faces marked with what they assumed were numbers. Vallow looked without much interest. Covington leaned over to look at a bench lined with the clocks. He pointed to one and waved to indicate his interest. The shopkeeper would not let him pick it up, but wound it for him and pressed a button on top to start it. A "second" hand went around busily while a larger hand moved across the half-circle.

"This isn't a time-of-day clock," Covington said. "It's a stop-watch, I mean a stop-clock."

"They all are," Wiegand said. "They all have the button on the side like that."

"Every time I see something normal around here," Covington complained, "something screwy like this happens a minute later. Why wouldn't a clock store sell regular clocks?"

"You know," Wiegand said thoughtfully, "I had one of those deals in college where I went to Germany for a month in my junior year, and I thought the same thing about Germans. Sometimes they seemed normal, like Americans, and then they'd get all foreign and European on me."

"Hell," Covington said, "I went up one time to the north shore suburbs and felt like that. I think our buddy here is getting bored. Maybe the clock stores in his neighborhood are exactly like this one."

"Let's keep going."

They sauntered up the street in the bright "sun" light, admiring girls in fancy hats and loose trousers, who often glanced sharply at their sombreros. "We have *got* to get rid of these hats," Covington said. "Either that, or actually become winos."

Vallow suddenly pointed ahead and walked fast, with the others behind him. He had found a bookstore, with untidy shelves of fairly normal-looking books out on the sidewalk. They were used books, to judge from the condition, and well-used at that. The proprietor was a shabby old man wearing exactly the same sombrero-like style of hat as the

Earthmen had, except even dirtier. He sat on a chair by the door and regarded them stolidly.

They searched for books with pictures, and found some with drawings and engraved plates, occasionally photography and color printing. Wiegand suddenly lifted a book high and grinned. "Here we go! This is what the doctor ordered!" It was clearly a children's dictionary, full of simple black and white pictures. One cover was ripped off, and the pages were ragged along the edges.

"You got any money?" Covington asked Vallow, pulling out the linings of the pockets in his short pants to indicate his meaning.

Vallow searched the pockets of his coverall. Unlike the Earthmen, he was carrying lots of stuff in several pockets. He pulled out an item and Covington gasped.

"That's a cell phone!" he said, pointing. "Or a pocket calculator, or a meter or anyway something electronic. This guy's a *long* way from home! Can I see that for a minute?" Vallow handed it over, and continued to search in his pockets.

Wiegand and Covington bent over to look at it. It was the size of a bar of soap, made of some material that appeared blue and white to Wiegand, and had a bank of slide switches on one side and what might have been an output window on the other. It didn't seem to be working.

Vallow discovered a small screwdriver that he was willing to give up. He showed it to the old man and pointed to the beat-up dictionary. It was a reasonable swap — the bookseller accepted the screwdriver for the book without getting up. Vallow took the book in his hand, but he was clearly more interested in the fact that the other two were deeply interested in his manufactured devices. He pulled out another, different palm-sized device, this one a short cylinder with sliding rings at the base, marked with graduated scales. He also had a pocket knife, a couple of other small tools, a little package of blank note cards and a nail clipper.

"Okay, he's not from Sad For," Wiegand said, "but of course we knew that already."

"He's either from a more advanced culture, or ..."

"Or his people have more money to buy toys than the people of good old Sad For can scrape up," Wiegand said. "This stuff is a lot more advanced than what they sell on this street."

Vallow pointed up into the sky. "It's getting dark," Covington said.

"We haven't been up more than four hours," Wiegand said.

"Still, I think it's sunset or the local equivalent."

The bookseller shooed them away and starting pulling the books inside his little shack. Vallow led the way back to the church mission building. It seemed to be a conviction with him that no one would stay out after dark. The other shops were closing as well.

"We seriously need to talk with this guy," Covington said. He borrowed the dictionary from Vallow and thumbed through it as they walked. "Here's a ball, and a chair, and some kind of monster and a big ... I don't know what that's supposed to be ... and a scissors. This book'll help a lot."

They arrived at the mission as the sky turned dark blue, and were admitted to the back room where they fell asleep quickly.

Chapter 5

In the morning Sad For Elkanicut returned to the mission. The clients ate porridge again, and then swept and cleaned the building. The preacher shooed them all outside to the street to join a dozen other men in a variety of rumpled hats, including several of the winos, who greeted Covington, Wiegand, and Vallow like old friends. Several of the carts with alien horses clop-clopped up and the drivers looked the crowd over.

An old man with gray-shot blue hair turned up his nose at the regular bums, many of whom he seemed to recognize personally, but was interested in the three foreigners. He had a spirited conversation with Elkanicut and passed him some coins, after which Elkanicut smiled brightly and indicated the three of them should get into the cart.

"Did we just get *sold?*" Wiegand asked.

"Maybe it's day labor," Covington said nervously. "Maybe they just pay a finder's fee to the mission or something."

"Should we make a run for it?"

Vallow noticed their expressions and patted them on the arms reassuringly. He apparently understood the situation even though he didn't speak the language. They climbed into the cart and the Earthmen felt obliged to follow. After a little more conversation, the old man snapped the reins and the beasts pulled the cart away.

The driver turned back to them, pointed to himself and introduced himself as "Sad For Belltria." He seemed to want to know everyone's names and waited for each of them to introduce himself. He corrected Vallow ("*Sad For* Vallow") when Vallow tried to give his name without the prefix.

"I suppose that's hopeful," Covington said. "You don't usually need to know names if you're just hauling cargo."

The "horses" paced up the street. The stores and tenements gave way to factories and warehouses, their names painted on the sides. There were more trucks on the road, none of them with passengers. They passed a road leading to the spaceport, and they watched as one of the spaceships lifted off and soared over the town like a balloon, to vanish among the clouds, arches and streamers in the sky. The ship was much larger than they had seen before. The hamburger-bun shape was easily three stories tall and wider than that across. It moved silently, with no clue as to its motive power.

"I'm guessing either the Cortay — Cortays? — anyway, the aliens run the spaceships, or Vallow's people do." Wiegand remarked. "The humans here sure don't have that level of technology."

"It looks like humans are allowed to drive trucks when they're working, but not to go joyriding around in them," Covington said. "That sucks."

"I get the impression humans aren't doing real well here-and-now."

"Yeah, clearly our job here is to start a big revolution, as soon as all these people realize we're here to save them. I can see the movie poster now."

"You think we're on a mission from God, like the Blues Brothers?"

"We'll have to steal a car first. Gotta have car chases for that," Covington said, grinning.

"Seriously, you think we're on a mission from God? Like we got put here by God for a purpose?"

"We did get put here for a purpose and we are on a mission from God," Covington said. "But we were back in Chicago, too. That's every day, for everybody. It'd do you good to get to church once in a while, amigo."

"Okay, don't get huffy on me."

"Pete," Covington said, "if you're going to get religion, you don't *start* with the weird stuff. That's for experts. Look, I'm a trained and experienced religious fanatic, so leave the irresponsible speculation to me. I got the chops for it and you don't."

"Deal. You tell me when it's time to go crazy and I'll take it from there. Seriously, did you ever want to study for the ministry?"

"Nope. I always wanted to be a scientist, and besides, I hated the idea that a preacher always has to do fund raising all the time. Then I got to be a scientist and guess what joy I was allowed to have?"

"Fund-raising?"

"Bingo."

"You did bingo for fund-raising?"

"Not for science, although now that you mention it I probably should have tried that. No, I had to wear a suit and be the brilliant ghetto kid who was going to save the world through metallurgy when the department talked to the donors. That *shtick* gets old after a while, you know?"

Sad For Belltria pulled the cart to a halt at the curb. Vallow stood up incautiously in the cart and looked around. They were in front of a tall wooden factory building with a wide door, but it was relatively dark inside compared to the sunlight-level brightness outdoors, and they could not see clearly within.

Belltria had dismounted so they got out too. Vallow spotted a broken piece of wood on the sidewalk, a finished beam like a two-by-four that had been shattered at one end into splinters, and immediately picked it up with the broken end upward. When he thrust it into the shadows, the individual splinters all lit up slightly and he was able to see a little better.

"He knew just what to do," Covington said, climbing out of the cart. "Obviously Vallow's from here, I mean this planet, just from another country or something."

"This place is a saw mill," Wiegand said. "Looks like a big old steam engine back there, and lots of lumber stacked up. I don't see the saw blade from here, but I bet that's what they do, is saw up trees and sell finished wood."

A middle-aged man stepped out into the light and greeted Belltria. They exchanged a little friendly banter, and Belltria introduced Vallow to him. Vallow did a little step-and-bow like a curtsey, apparently a custom of his own country which the two locals found comical. The factory man found him acceptable, and he waved cheerfully to Wiegand and Covington as they vanished into the gloom of the sawmill. Vallow was carrying the dictionary.

Belltria did not get back into the cart. Instead, he pointed to a much smaller wooden building next door. It was a restaurant, a lunch-counter kind of place with hand-painted signs taped to the window. He led Covington and Wiegand inside.

The place was empty except for one man sitting by himself at a table reading a newspaper by the "sunlight" through the window. They assumed it must not be a meal time. There were about a dozen tables with chairs, a counter at the front where the diners apparently stood up to eat, and a station by the door with a till drawer but no mechanical cash register. Belltria introduced them to a plump, pretty young woman named Sad For Jarhon, the cashier, who wore a hat decorated with flowers and smiled nicely for them. There was a middle-aged male waiter named Sad For Eebeer and in the kitchen, a beefy male cook named Sad For Sembelyan.

Belltria steered them toward the sink in the kitchen and pointed to huge stacks of dirty dishes. "We've been typecast!" Covington said. "He must have talked to the minister."

"Apparently we're the Pearl Divers," Wiegand said.

Covington turned on the water and started filling the sink, and located dish soap (a different brand) and wash rags. "Okay, boss man," he said to Belltria. "We get it." To Wiegand he said, "I'll start out washing again but we're going to trade off, right?"

"Sure, sure. Are these supposed to be clean drying towels?" Wiegand held up the damp, dirty towels to Belltria, who opened a cabinet to show him where the fresh towels were. Belltria also pointed out where the pots, pans and tableware were stored, and the cook hauled over a huge, messy pot and dropped it with a clang on the sink counter. Then they left the Earthmen to their own devices.

"This'll be a good educational situation," Covington said.

"How do you mean?"

"Did you see the menu board out in the main room? Those have got to be the names of dishes they serve and the prices. Once we can match the food to a line on the menu, we start learning how to read and also we learn about their system of arithmetic. It's like the Rosetta Stone with cheeseburgers."

"Greasy cheeseburgers, judging from these pans," Wiegand said. "Okay, it's a living."

They worked steadily for a couple of hours, reducing the pile of dirty dishes considerably, until Belltria called everyone together for lunch. There were no customers in the dining room, so everyone gathered at a table and took sandwiches from a big plate Sembelyan brought out. He also brought out a pitcher of drink and glasses.

"Hey!" Wiegand said. "That looks like *beer!*" He took a cautious sip, then smiled. "My God, it *is* beer, sort of. Or something equivalent, I suppose. It's even cold. It has foam. Life is good."

"Thank you, Jesus!" Covington said. He, Jarhon and Belltria paused to say a quick grace over their meal — Covington prayed looking down, the others prayed looking up — and Covington took a sip himself. "Not real good beer," he said, "but I'll take it." With some gestures, he was able to establish that the local word for the drink was "carror" and he smiled, waved the glass around and repeated it.

The sandwiches were good also, and they were able to learn the name of the sandwich and point to it on the menu. Covington was asking about "plate", "glass", "fork" (sporks were not used at this establishment) and so forth, taking the opportunity to talk to pretty Jarhon rather than the men. Wiegand suddenly interrupted.

"I've got a color!" he cried. "I see this beer as yellow with white foam. Everything else is still blue and white, but the beer has a color. Maybe I'm getting my eyes back."

"I guess your brain has decided that if that's beer, whatever color it has must be yellow," Covington said. "Is anything else yellow?"

Wiegand looked around, then pointed to a poster on the wall. "The oval behind that slogan, or name, or whatever it is in the corner. That's yellow, too."

"Everything still looks red and white to me but maybe I'll get colors back, too," Covington said.

Two men walked in and Belltria jumped up to seat them. Lunch was over: they cleared off the table and everyone went back to work.

The lunch-hour (if that was what it was) rush started and the restaurant filled up and stayed full for a couple of hours. Wiegand washed and Covington rinsed, dried and stacked, trying to keep up with the load. Sembelyan cooked steadily, working like a machine, with Belltria making sandwiches and plating the food beside him. Eebeer appeared every minute or two, either carrying trays out or bringing them in, and as well as the Earthmen could see without leaving the sink, Jarhon worked the till and also handled the stand-up counter.

The customers were mostly men, showing up in sudden groups of co-workers who knew each other and talked loudly through their meals. The occasional women who patronized the restaurant appeared in groups and generally would not enter unless they could get a table to themselves. The atmosphere was cheerful and crude, and the place smelled like sweat. Clearly the men were working hard at whatever they did.

In the "afternoon" (there was no change in the light from the sky, as far as they could see) the work slacked off again. Belltria came around and gave Covington and Wiegand each two small coins and indicated they could take a break. He led them out the back door to a cluttered yard set off from an alley by a wooden fence. There was a small wooden shack tilted against the back wall of the restaurant building. Belltria opened the creaking door, pointed his two dishwashers inside, then left them.

The shack had two cots with worn blankets, and one beat-up chair. "I guess the job comes with room and board," Covington said.

"Two cents a day, beer and sandwiches, and our own chicken coop," Wiegand said. "We're livin' large now, boy."

"I was afraid we weren't going to get paid at all."

"Slaves? Yeah, it could have been. But I think we can resign this luxury job any time and old Belltria just goes and fetches another couple of winos from the rescue mission. In fact, I'm sure that's what happened to the last guys."

"We should clean this place up a little," Covington said. "I'll go get the broom and stuff."

"Yeah, let's make it look nice. If I bring a girl back here, you're going to be a good roommate and go study at the library, right?"

"Sure thing, roomie. If you can find a girl you can take out for two cents and bring home to a chicken coop, ask her if she's got a sister, okay?"

"Aw, look on the bright side," Wiegand said. "We've got a crib, we get paid, we've got jobs as dishwashers. Our status has improved."

"How do you mean?"

"Back in Chicago, we were *postdocs*, dude."

"Good point." They swept and cleaned.

Chapter 6

Before they could finish cleaning up the shack, Belltria came out to bring them back for another meal rush (supper? second lunch? tea?) and they worked steadily for hours. At the end, all of the dishes were clean, but they were exhausted and cranky when darkness came and they finally reeled to bed.

Breakfast, when the dawn came, was another bowl of the oatmeal-like stuff. There was running water in the restaurant, but no shower, so they had to wash themselves as well as they could with a bucket of water, dish soap and rags. Covington came back into the restaurant without his sombrero just as Sad For Jarhon walked in the door, and she was shocked to see his naked head — or at least, felt that it was ladylike to appear shocked. She scrunched her eyes while he went back and fetched his hat.

They learned more nouns, the numerals used in prices, a few verbs such as "washing dishes" (which turned out to be a different verb than the one for washing yourself, or washing the floor), and a phrase which clearly meant "Get back to work!"

After they had finished all the dishes from the breakfast rush, Belltria allowed them to go back to their shack and resume cleaning it up with mops. As they were working, the sky began to darken.

Belltria conscientiously came outside, paid them their daily wages of two cents and left just as darkness fell.

"Brian," Wiegand said, "this day wasn't three hours long."

"The days and nights are irregular here," Covington said. "That's terrific. That really puts the cherry on the sundae, doesn't it? I *thought* yesterday must have been twenty or thirty hours long. Holy crap, how can that possibly work?"

"I have seriously got to sleep," Wiegand said. "Even though it's only been three hours."

"Me, too. Oh, man, as soon as you said that, the sleepiness hit. You know, I'll bet humans here are evolved to sleep whenever it gets dark and be active all day, no matter how long or short it is."

"Well, it's working on me. Good night."

"G'night, Pete." They lay down on their cots, and were asleep in minutes.

Each "day", the restaurant opened for business about an hour after dawn, whenever that came. Covington and Wiegand washed dishes until the morning rush was over, then swept and mopped the floor in the dining room and kitchen, and were on their own until the lunch rush. If the day continued, there would be a supper rush as well and on one nerve-wracking day, there were a total of five meal rushes before blessed night came. Belltria kept one of the stop-watch clocks on a shelf next to the till, and re-started it after each meal rush. The clock ticked off two and a half to three and a half major divisions on its scale between meals: they decided to call that period an "hour".

Belltria paid them two pennies each "day," meaning the period between two sleeps, no matter how long or short it was.

On the fourth day, Vallow came through the alley from the next-door sawmill during the afternoon break. He had about the same vocabulary in the local language as the Earthmen, a few dozen words, along with the words pictured in the children's dictionary, which he was glad to share. He was cheerful and friendly, and Wiegand and Covington found him immensely good to see. Wiegand had already scrounged a few chipped glasses, and while they could not get anywhere near the beer supply, they did have a bucket of clean water to share. In turn, the other went back to the sawmill for a few minutes and returned with some scrap wood they could use to make a couple of rude benches. The three of them had a fine time in the back yard by the alley, making broken conversation and toasting each other with glasses of water.

The next afternoon, while Wiegand and Covington were policing up the litter in the back, Vallow returned, this time with a woman co-worker. She had slightly curly hair, a little lighter than most people in Sad For. Her face was round and she had a wide generous smile, and wore a hat like a sunbonnet. She was as muscular as all the natives of the planet seemed to be. Vallow introduced her as Sad For Indarya.

Now the gathering was a party. After getting liquored up on two glasses of water, Vallow, who apparently fancied himself a ladies' man, stood up and danced a jig from his homeland, with many bows to Indarya. Covington drummed on the bench with a piece of wood for rhythm.

Everyone applauded. Covington stood and sang "I'm Going with Jesus All the Way," stepping and clapping. Indarya provided the drumming and after a while joined in on the chorus without understanding any of the words. Wiegand still had no rhythm but sang anyway.

Belltria and Sembelyan looked out the door to see what all the noise was about, then withdrew. Apparently it wasn't time to go back to work yet.

Vallow pulled out the children's dictionary and handed it to Indarya, who laughed at the sight. She cheerfully gestured for all of them to sit at her feet like good little children, and they played along. She taught them words page by page.

When she happened to reach the word and picture for "coin" (unless it meant "money" or that particular value of coin), Wiegand pulled out two pennies and showed them around. Everybody laughed, and Vallow displayed four of the same coins.

"They get paid four cents?" Wiegand asked. "Apparently, Belltria is taking our palatial room and board out of our salary." At that moment Belltria himself stuck his head out the back door, gave them a suspicious look on hearing his name, and spoke the sentence they knew: "Get back to work." Indarya and Vallow went back to the sawmill.

In between hours at the sink, Covington and Wiegand learned the names of all the sandwiches and dishes served at the restaurant, they learned numbers in the local notation, and they scrounged newspapers left behind by customers. They both gradually regained their color vision. The sky was still blue with bright white arches and domes, in Wiegand's eyes. But people had tan skins and black, brown or blonde hair, bread was brown and the sandwich fillings were various shades of green, including the food they thought of as meat. Beer was yellow, and they got a glass with lunch each day.

"Did you see those kids playing ball in the street this morning?" Wiegand asked, while drying dishes.

"Yeah. At least that's normal," Covington said. "It looked like exactly the kind of Calvin-ball we used to do. You know, throw the ball and argue about the rules."

"Actually, it wasn't normal at all."

"Pete, I seriously don't need any more weirdness for the rest of the day, or maybe for the rest of the week if they have weeks here."

"I've gotta tell you this," Wiegand said. "Some of those kids were running around with no shirts on. We haven't seen anybody else without shirts so far except ourselves."

"Okay, so?"

"So we don't have bellybuttons and they don't have bellybuttons either. Do you think *everybody* here gets born in the mud in a swamp?"

"Now that you mention it," Covington said slowly, "here's another one I just noticed. I've been washing dishes all morning." He held up his hands. "My fingers aren't wrinkly. They should be."

"Kiss my not-entirely-human butt. You're right."

Covington wiped his hands on a towel, then looked down to pray. "Father God, I'm trying to cope with this but I need Your help, I need Your love, I've got too much weird stuff to deal with here, this is driving me crazy. God, I know You'll get me through this, and I thank You, God. Amen."

"Let me know if He tells you anything," Wiegand said. "Because God knows I don't have a clue."

"No bellybuttons. We drink this liquid and wash dishes in it but I'm starting to think maybe this isn't really water," Covington mused. "We're low-budget *Star Trek* aliens, but women are pretty much regular nice women, and beer is beer. They have normal things like newspapers and soap and dirty dishes. On the other hand, days and nights are totally whack, the sky is strange, the glowing-pointy-thing I can't figure out at all, and there's those bones-on-the-outside alien horses, not to mention the aliens with no heads. Where does that leave us?"

"Washing dishes. Suppose it would help if I pray for enlightenment too?"

"The fruit of the Spirit is love, joy, peace, patience, kindness, goodness, faithfulness, gentleness and self-control," Covington quoted. "If you get some of that stuff from Him, you're a worshiper. If you get physics or biology or something, you're a twit. God gives me a lot of gifts, but I never did get Him to do my homework for me. We're going to have to figure this out ourselves."

"I imagine you miss having a Bible, eh?"

"You bet. I miss my family and my girlfriend and my church. I miss pizza and I really, really miss Google. I didn't realize how soft my brain had gotten from being able to look things up instantly."

"Hey, we're done with the lunch dishes! Thank you, Jesus!"

"Pete," Covington said, "don't say that, okay? When I say it, I mean it. You don't."

"Sorry."

The restaurant was quiet. Eebeer the waiter had gone out, and Sad For Jarhon was sitting on a stool at the counter reading a newspaper. There was only one customer in the dining room, a portly young man reading a book in the light that poured through the window. He had a cup of the local tea and a plate of biscuits, and two more books on the table. Belltria did not like his staff to clean up when there were customers, but obviously he did not expect this man to leave any time soon. He told them to go ahead. Covington cleaned the tops of the tables with a rag while Wiegand went to fill the mop bucket.

The stacked dishes in the back room began to rattle.

Jarhon leaped off her stool, her eyes wild. "Everybody out!" Belltria yelled, and Wiegand and Sembelyan ran out from the back. Covington leaped to the front door and held it open, unable to think of anything more useful. The man at the table grabbed up his books, spilling one, and rushed out with the rest. Everyone was out on the street by the time the hanging pans began clanging together.

The shaking of the ground was really only slightly stronger than what would be caused by a heavy truck passing. Every building on the street contributed a rattling and creaking noise as the doors flew open and the panicky people raced out. A flood of men and women ran out of the factory which was across from the restaurant, and from the saw mill next door.

The tremor passed quickly. A moment later they were all looking at each other, and then everyone started talking.

Wiegand tried to ask Belltria if earthquakes or tremors were common. What he actually said was, "This (he swept his hand around) it does many?"

"It's been happening since [something]," Belltria said. "Not bad here, so far. But getting worse."

Sad For Jarhon started a story, apparently about a relative who had lost everything in an earthquake (judging by her extravagant expressions). Neither of the Earthmen could make much of it at the speed she was talking, and the others appeared to have heard the story already.

"These people are pretty skittish," Covington said to Wiegand. "I think they've been through this before."

"Well, you heard Belltria," Wiegand said. "I don't know when he was trying to tell me this started, but I guess it didn't used to happen."

"Yeah. I'm sure they felt the earthquake that hatched us — that town wasn't that far away. Probably around here it was just another tremor."

"Come to think of it, that newspaper we looked at yesterday, that had a picture of a damaged town."

The excitement died down when the temblor did not reoccur. "I guess the show's over," Covington said. "But I don't see anybody rushing to go back inside. Looks like that one customer we had went home on his own."

"I don't suppose it would hurt that much if the chicken coop fell over," Wiegand said. "But if the back wall of the building falls on us, we're toast. Or maybe I should say we're pancakes."

"Thanks so much for sharing that, Pete. You realize we don't have any place else to sleep tonight, right? Sweet dreams."

"One thing I'll say for this place. After the first night, I haven't had any trouble sleeping through the night. Whether it's two hours or twenty, I just conk right out."

"Me too. It's kind of obvious people here aren't exactly *homo sapiens*. They're obviously evolved to live on irregular sleep. I think they don't even have the *concept* of sitting up to watch the *Late Show* on TV, even if they had TV's."

"Which they don't," Wiegand said.

Vallow and Indarya were among the crowd from the saw mill. Now they saw the Earthmen and waved, then walked over.

"Hello, Indarya," Covington said. "Hello, Vallow."

"Sad For Indarya," she corrected him, smiling.

"Sorry. *Sad For* Indarya," he said. He waved around him. "Sad For?"

"This is Sad For," she said.

"'Sad' means?"

She pointed to houses and buildings along the street. "House, house, building, house, building," she said, then spread her arms to indicate them all and said "Sad!"

"I guess that means 'city' or 'town'," Covington said in English. "Okay, how about 'for'?" He looked at her and asked "For?"

She seemed at a loss about how to explain, then reached into a pocket of her long trousers and pulled out some coins. One of them was noticeably newer and shinier than the others. She pointed to that one and said "for", then pointed to the others and said the word for "no".

"'For' is 'new'," Wiegand said. "I get it!" Apparently Vallow had the same burst of understanding because he started chattering to Indarya in his limited language. "'Sad For' is 'Town New'. We're in New Town!"

Covington said "Thank you" to Indarya, then turned to Wiegand. "And I guess it's important that we call her 'New Town Indarya' rather than plain Indarya."

"Do you suppose nobody else in New Town is named 'Indarya'?" Wiegand asked. "I guess the name of your town could sort of substitute for a family name in that case. That means the place where we were, you know, like born was 'Dogat'. But the people there wouldn't let us use the name 'Dogat'."

By this time, the crowd in the street was thinning as people drifted back to their houses and workplaces. Belltria came up to them and said, "Take a break, we won't need you until [something]."

"Thank you," Covington said to him, and to Wiegand, "I guess we're off for a while." With a combination of gestures and his meager stock of words, he invited the others to come back with them to their backyard for a gathering.

"We'd like that," Indarya said, catching Vallow by eye. They went through the front door of the restaurant, heading for the back. But Wiegand suddenly went over to the table by the window where their customer had sat, and fetched a book that had fallen to the floor.

"That guy's a regular," he said. "We can give this back to him tomorrow." They went out into the back yard, and Covington served water and also brought out a plate of clean food scraps they had thoughtfully salvaged from customer's plates.

"The guy must be a teacher," Wiegand said, flipping pages in the book. "Look at the pictures here. I think this is a science textbook, maybe for a high school. Kind of a general science book, I think, or anyway it covers a lot of different stuff."

"Oh, man," Covington said, and Vallow jumped up to peer over Wiegand's shoulder. He urgently gestured to see the book, then flipped pages himself. After a moment, he proudly held the book out for them all to look at one page.

"The simple machines!" Covington said. "Inclined plane, lever, screw, pulleys." Vallow also grinned and said a string of words, probably the names of the same devices in his own language.

"Man, talk about meeting an old friend!" Wiegand said. "We did this unit in high school. The drawings look pretty much the same as I remember, too. Of course, they'd have to, I guess."

Covington had taken the book back. "No, I don't think they'd necessarily be the same. There's something screwy about the physics here. But you're right, this looks pretty much exactly the way we had it in my high school, too. This is our key to the whole world, right here."

"Can I see it again?" Wiegand said. He took the book back, and the other men looked over his shoulder. Indarya sat on the bench and smiled at them indulgently.

"Here's the inclined plane," Wiegand said, pointing with his finger. "Somewhere here, it's got to say that resistance over effort equals length over height. This string is right below the picture and it's in seven parts. So let's say the little cokebottle in the middle is equality. Ay yup, here's another one in the middle of an expression, and ... yeah, okay, that's the equals sign. Then this squiggle has to be 'divided-by' and this one is multiplication. We're cookin' now. I bet I could actually do some of these homework problems."

"You solved that pretty fast," Covington said.

"Comes from being a Perl programmer," Wiegand said modestly. "Stand back, because I just might feel the need to use a regular expression."

Vallow was obviously also enthralled to see the familiar diagrams. But Wiegand suddenly felt embarrassed that Indarya was left out of the conversation. He handed the book to Vallow and sat down beside her, but she stood up and took the book away from Vallow with a smile, then sat back down with it.

She leafed through the book, passing pictures of strange animals and plants, a page that showed a chemistry lab with wonderfully familiar beakers and retorts, pictures of rocks and other general-science stuff. Finally she found a section with a color photograph of a planet from space. It looked enough like Earth, blue and white with oceans and continents, to give Wiegand a rush of homesickness. She flipped past this and found a gallery of a dozen other planet pictures, many of them also Earth-like. She pointed to one and said, "This is Brythe." She reached down to pat the ground and said again, "This is Brythe."

She handed the book to Wiegand and asked, "Where are you from?"

He said, "Earth." He did not point to a picture.

She looked at him skeptically, then handed the book to Vallow and asked him the same question. He carefully scanned all the pictures, then gave a very ordinary shrug. He said, "Valsket Innopa." He also did not point to a picture, and Indarya looked sharply at them all.

"There's, what, seven different Earth-like planets on that page," Covington said in English. "Or at least, blue and white planets that look right. We're not from any of them and apparently our friend isn't either."

"Where are you from?" Wiegand asked Indarya, repeating her words.

She patted the ground again and said, "Brythe. This is my world."

Belltria came out to tell them to go back to work. Covington passed the open book to him and asked him the same question. He paged back to the first, larger picture. "Home," he said. "If I can make enough money with this restaurant, I'm going back there. Come on, work to do."

*   *   *

That night there was another temblor. It was no stronger than the previous one, but the Earthmen awoke from the clattering and rattling in the kitchen, and ran out the back way, through the alley and back out to the street. There was a much smaller crowd of people standing in the street, sleepy and mostly silent. Some of them carried pointed metal rods that flared like candles when held upright. In the dark, Wiegand saw that the pointed roofs of the buildings twinkled faintly at the crests.

They stood looking up at the dim arches in the black night sky. There were some pale moving lights, but no moon and no stars. One of the silent spaceships drifted overhead on its way toward the spaceport.

After a while, when the rumble had passed away, they went back to their shack and slept again through the night.

Chapter 7

The owner of the science book came back the next morning, and ordered biscuits and tea as he usually did. He was round-faced and studious, balding on top although the ruff of hair on his spine was still copious, and jotted in a notebook as he read. After finishing the breakfast dishes, the Earthmen brought the book back to him, and tried to convey that they'd like to read more.

"Do you want it?" he asked. "If I give it to you, will you read it? Seriously, you actually *want* to read it? It's yours, it's yours, take it!" He thrust it back to them, grinning.

"We don't talk how you talk very good," Covington said. "New to here. Thank you. Thank you."

The man looked at Covington, then tried a sentence in a different language. When that got no response, he tried again in a third language, one with tonal shifts that gave it a sing-song effect.

"What planet are you from?" he asked in the common language. When Covington and Wiegand discussed that with each other in English, he broke in to say "What's that you're speaking?"

"It is our way to talk on our planet," Wiegand said haltingly.

"'Language'," he said, giving them the local word. "It means how to talk. But there are only two planets with different languages."

"Our planet is 'Earth'," Covington said.

He looked at them both sharply, started to speak, then thought better of it. Finally he said, "My name is Gron Orrata Hemmet Card."

"Sad For Peter Wiegand."

"Sad For Brian Covington."

"You're not from Sad For," Card said. "Why not name yourself 'Earth Breen Covton' if you're from this 'Earth' place?"

"Brian Covington," Covington corrected him. "I ... we live here, now, in Sad For."

"I live in Sad For, too, until I can get out," Card said. "But there's no way I would ever call myself 'Sad For Card'." He relaxed and smiled again, and tried to talk.

With some pantomiming and pointing, they established that he was a teacher, that he did not teach children but older students, that he considered his students dummies and that he was glad to find anyone at all who wanted to read books and learn.

Card pulled out a blank sheet of paper and drew them a rough map, starting from the street the restaurant was on and leading to a building closer to the center of town. "Come and see me [something]."

"Thank you," Covington said. "But we have to work."

"Not [something]," Card said. When they looked at him blankly, he said "Four days".

"Oh! All right, four days, thank you, thank you," Wiegand said. To Covington, in English, he said, "I wonder if that's Sunday again."

"I was sure hoping we'd get a day off sooner or later."

"Good," Card said. "But I have to go to work now, myself." He gathered up his other books and left the restaurant. Wiegand and Covington went back to mopping the floor.

For three afternoons, they studied the book in the back yard with Vallow, who obviously had a technical education. Two men would read and discuss the book, and one would always make time to sit with Sad For Indarya.

"It's good of you to come out here with us," Wiegand said to her, while Covington talked to Vallow about a chapter on geology.

"I like it, I like you all," Indarya said. They were sitting together on the rude bench. "In the factory I'm just the girl who pushes a broom. Out here, I'm the little queen and you are my subjects."

Wiegand stood and bowed first, then knelt in front of her. "Command me anything, my queen," he said. "You can have anything sixteen cents can buy."

"Silly," she said. "Besides, if I were queen I'd buy *you* gifts, starting with a new hat."

"Are these hats as bad as Brian thinks?"

"Sad For Brian," she corrected him absently. "Yes, they are. I'll ask around home to see if anyone has some old hats. They'd be better than what you've got. You look like [somethings]."

"What does that mean?"

She stuck out her thumb and little finger and mimed drinking from a jug. Wiegand laughed. "Why is it so important to say 'Sad For' Brian instead of just his name?" he asked.

"If you just call him 'Brian'," she said, "that would mean he is a person who does not belong to any group. People would think that was because no group would have him, and that would be a very rude thing to say."

"You have to belong to a group?"

"You can't be a whole person all by yourself," she said promptly. It sounded like a proverb.

Wiegand considered that a moment. "What is 'Gron Orrata Hemmet'?" he asked. "The man who gave us that book is called that."

"I know what 'Gron Orrata' is, anyway," Indarya said. "It's a big college." They had some hand-waving to explain that term. "It's on Home. Very old, very good. He must be smart."

"*Home* is a planet?"

"Home is the planet of humans, where we all came from in the beginning. Most people here came from Home, although I was born here. You can tell by my big muscles."

"I *thought* everybody here looked strong," Wiegand said. "Why?"

"Because we are heavier on Brythe than on Home. People from Home come here and are very tired until they get stronger. Fat rich people" — she held her hands out in front of her belly — "from Home come here to lose weight. People who are born here have nice big muscles." She flexed her arm and guided Wiegand's hand to her bicep, flirting with him. "Feel the muscle."

Wiegand tried to do a wolf whistle in appreciation but discovered he could not make his still-unfamiliar tongue and teeth do it. He settled for a smile.

Covington drifted over, and Wiegand recapped what he had learned, in English. "Apparently, you get to pick whatever prefix you want for your name, and Card never got over being the local equivalent of a Yalie. I wonder how long it's been since he left his Ivy league school? I bet he feels like he's been sent to the sticks, here."

"Hell, that was written all over him," Covington said. "So Home has lower gravity? We could go there and be Superman or John Carter or somebody. Cool!"

"I don't think it's that much difference. She says they have fat farms here where people from Home come to lose weight."

"That's data," Covington said thoughtfully. "That means it doesn't cost such a lot to fly here, if you can come here and go back after a month."

"Sad For Indarya," Covington said to her, in her language, "do people come here in ships like this?" He drew an outline of the hamburger-bun ships in the dirt with a stick.

"Yes. The Cortays run them. I've never been on one myself."

"How much does it cost?"

She considered. "Well, I knew a girl who went to Home when she got married, and the guy she married didn't have much money. It costs more than I have, anyway," she said finally, and smiled shyly. "But I don't make very much money."

"More than us, I think," Wiegand said gallantly.

"Well ..." Indarya said delicately, and let it drop there.

The next day, Indarya showed up with three well-used hats, like narrow-brimmed fedoras with a flat crown, multi-colored in shades of blue and brown. She put them on her men and stood back to admire the results. "There," she said, "you don't look like winos any more. Tilt the hat this way. Yes! That looks handsome."

"Are these new?" Vallow asked. "Should we pay you for them?"

"No, no, they're so old nobody wears that style any more," Indarya said. "I got them from my father's friends. But now you look like poor young men who can't afford a new hat, instead of bums. You look very [something] — that's good!"

"What should be do with the old hats?"

"We'll give them to the church for the poor," she said. "That's how you got them."

With Indarya's help over the next two days, and a newspaper left behind in the restaurant, they were able to establish that there were eight or nine human planets in the local empire or confederation or whatever it was. There was also one Cortay planet and one inhabited by "The Hands of God," (with much hand-waving to explain that name), which no one was allowed to visit. Indarya had a vague idea that there were also some other planets not used by anybody.

"What are the Hands of God?" Covington asked.

"You talk to them at church if you have problems," Indarya said. "They tell you what to do. They're very nice."

"What do they look like?"

"Nobody has ever seen one. They just talk to us, all you hear is their voice. They help us all the time. They teach us about God."

"Hmm. Well, we'll see you later."

"Flow with it," Indarya said as she left.

"I don't know about you," Covington said to Wiegand later that day, while washing dishes, "but that raises a flag for me. That sounds like some kind of advanced non-humans who are lording it over the humans."

"Could be," Wiegand said. "On the other hand, she said nobody's ever seen one, so maybe this is just the priests telling everybody they get messages from angels."

"Yeah, if you were going to have angels in your theology, I could see putting them on a planet nobody can get to. You know, I want to go to this church if we ever get a day off. I mean, assuming the day off is the day they have church services."

"Tomorrow," Wiegand said. "That's when Card invited us over. By the way, I talked to him yesterday while you were working in here and he repeated that invitation. I think he's lonely."

"Well, let's go talk to Mr. Ivy League and then maybe I'll go to church, if I can find where it is."

"You going to be okay going to this church? I mean, they can't be Christians. I don't know how big of a deal that is for you."

"I think it'll be okay," Covington said. "Assuming this planet is real and not some kind of video game, I wouldn't expect the church to be anything familiar. But when we were strangers, they fed us. They gave us those hip, hot and happenin' sombreros, so they get points for that. Besides, it's the only game in town, as far as I know. I kind of need to get together with the saints, you know?"

"Not me. I need a day off with no dishwashing and no commitments. You go to church and I'll just goof off. But listen, if it turns out they're the kind of church that has crazy fertility rites with bongo drums, come get me, okay? For that, I could get religion."

"Don't hold your breath, amigo."

Chapter 8

The next day, after an unusually long night, *was* the equivalent of Sunday. The restaurant was closed, although Belltria had said nothing to them. Wiegand and Covington had thoughtfully saved up enough table scraps to keep them fed for a day, but were unable to enjoy the luxury of sleeping late: their Brythean bodies seemed adapted to waking immediately on "sunrise," whenever it was.

It had rained during the night, and the streets were wet and puddled when the two stepped out of the backyard and onto the street, wearing their new hats. The sky was covered by a thick gray overcast of stratus clouds, which made the town seem less strange. The factories were straightforward, the white wooden houses only a little odd, and the umbrella-carrying people on the street were beginning to look entirely ordinary to them except that the tips of the umbrellas glowed. They followed the wooden sidewalk toward the center of New Town.

They passed a group of children playing a game with a ball in an empty lot, shouting and laughing as they kicked the ball through the puddles and wet grass and got themselves spattered with dots of mud in the process. The tips of the grass sparkled through drops of water. "Looks like soccer, sort of," Wiegand commented.

"Except they're allowed to push and shove each other, unless that's just kids being kids," Covington said. One of the boys accidentally kicked the ball off-sides toward them.

Wiegand grinned and said, "I'm about to turn into my grandpa." He stopped the ball with one foot and said in Polish-accented English, "Here, kid, let me show you how we used to do it back in the old country," then repeated that as well as he could in the local language. He popped the ball from one foot to the other a few times, then shuffled the ball forward a few steps between his feet and kicked it accurately back. The boy laughed and waved.

A junk wagon came down the street toward them, driven by an old man wearing a hat much like theirs and pulled by one of the alien "horses". The animal was old, too, judging from the scarred and weathered appearance of the exterior bones that formed its skeleton. It plodded wearily past them, turning its round head to regard them successively with three of its four small eyes. The driver barely gave them a glance.

"You and Vallow get anywhere with the science book yesterday?" Wiegand asked as they walked.

"Yeah, some," Covington said, "while you were schmoozing with Indarya."

"I was working on my language skills."

"Sure you were. Anyway, the geology section looked pretty much okay as near as I could tell. There was a section on chemistry which I couldn't make heads or tails of, although it didn't seem to bother Vallow. I couldn't find any formulas I recognized. Same thing with the section on electricity — he was okay with it, I was confused. The chapter on machines had gears and pulleys, all normal, and we were looking at something about an internal combustion motor that looked pretty antique but no stranger than you'd see in an old magazine."

"The math seemed pretty normal, once you get the notation," Wiegand said. "I found some trig and log tables, nothing very advanced."

"Yeah. You know that section we looked at with pictures of the planets? There wasn't one diagram in there with anything that looked like an orbit." Both of them sighed.

"So anyway, Vallow for sure went to some college, obviously not the one Card went to, or he'd speak the language."

"Some college where they use a different system of math," Wiegand said. "He was at least as confused as I was."

"Hmm."

"Also, back in his college, he was captain of the rowing crew or the Quidditch team or the Skee-Ball Club or whatever they had," Wiegand said. "I can tell a jock when I see one. He looks pretty dapper in his hat, too. Me, I look like a guy wearing a hat."

"Oh, settle down," Covington said airily. "It isn't given to all of us to be nerds, you know. Besides, Indarya seems pretty sensible. She wouldn't throw herself at a handsome jock."

"You're *not* helping."

The stores they passed were mostly open, and apparently they did look more prosperous, because many of the storekeepers, lounging in their doorways, urged them to come in. Several of the bars were open. Just for curiosity, they entered one reasonably clean tavern and looked around. It seemed ordinary enough — there were a half-dozen square tables with chairs, two of them occupied by drinkers building up an early-morning load — and a counter where a bartender stood by a barrel of beer and a few bottles of other liquors, washing glasses in a sink. Covington asked him the price of a glass of beer and held out his palm with a few of Belltria's pennies. The bartender sourly used one finger to move two of the pennies to one side. They thanked him politely and left without buying.

"A day's pay for one beer?" Wiegand said outside. "Obviously, we're not going to be able to afford to be alcoholics here."

"Ol' Belltria's getting a pretty good deal for his two cents wages. Still, where else are we going to go?"

"Well, that's the leverage he has on us, isn't it?"

The city center, when they reached it, had a few substantial buildings of brick, with walk-ups up to four stories. The streets were better paved, there were trees in planters, and some of the people were dressed more formally. Many of the men wore robes and a particular style of wide-brimmed hats, although still with short pants. Fashionable women wore capes, which they seemed to like to swirl dramatically, over bright-colored tunics and long trousers. Covington spotted the central church, a large building with textures picked out in fancy brickwork, tall windows and a serene courtyard with trees on one side. The river symbol was formed on the wall in shiny metal next to the carved wooden doors.

But Card's college, when they found it, was a collection of three two-story wood buildings painted an unattractive dun color, with a lawn between them divided into smaller patches by dusty trails pounded out by students. Under the gray sky, it seemed deserted and forlorn — apparently students did not live on-campus and were home for the sabbath.

They picked out the door specified in Card's instructions. It was not locked. They let themselves into a brown-painted hallway with classroom doors on either side. Card's lab was in the middle of the building. They knocked on his door, and he let them in with a smile.

"Welcome, welcome," he said, waving them in. "I've got the drink of all scientists — tea brewed in a flask over a gas burner — so help yourselves. I think you *were* scientists back home?"

"Yes, we were," Wiegand said. They poured themselves tea in ordinary-looking teacups and sat on stools along one lab bench. The lab was so familiar and ordinary it made them homesick. There were stone-topped benches with sinks, with enough stools to hold perhaps two dozen students. The black counters on each side of the room were filled with shelves, and a dozen microscopes in dust covers were lined up by the windows. There were balances and test tube racks, posters of dissected plants and animals, and a full-size skeleton hanging from a rack at one end, which they walked over to see. It was fairly close to what they expected a human skeleton to look like, but some of the hip bones and others were odd.

"You're part of the general science department?" Covington asked, making conversation.

"I am the entire general science department," Card said bitterly. "In fact, I'm the only teacher in the only science department."

"What do they teach here?" Wiegand asked.

They didn't have the words to understand the answer until Card pulled out an illustrated booklet (the catalog, perhaps?) and pointed to the pictures. "Machine repair, agriculture, office work, surveying," he said. "Nothing that calls for very much science, or much of any background, really. The students we get, they couldn't handle much more real education anyway."

"Ah." There didn't seem to be much to add to that.

"It's just nice to meet someone who has an education," Card went on. "I get so tired of trying to get these wood-heads interested in anything. They wouldn't have lasted a day back in my own college."

He gave them a sharp look. "But I'm also interested in where you gentlemen came from. There are twelve Home-like planets in the Home Space. Of the nine that are inhabited, two speak different languages given to them by the Hands of God. All the rest speak the same language we have here. Now we have two young men who speak a different language. We have often thought there are other human planets elsewhere in the universe, and I suspect you two are from one of these planets." He paused, then continued, "How am I doing?" He sat back in triumph.

Covington said slowly, "Pete and I are not from another planet in your universe, I don't think."

"So you just fell out of the sky, then?"

"You're making fun of us, but as far as we know, that's about it."

"Hmm." Card stood up, slightly unstable, and walked to a cabinet along one wall. He pulled open the wooden door, holding on to the handle as he leaned too far back. "Brian," Wiegand whispered, "the guy's a little drunk."

"Ya think? I can smell him."

Card came back carrying a wooden case with a handle on top. He unfastened some clips and lifted off the top and sides to reveal an open cubical frame of metal. Thin vertical wires held painted wooden beads in various fixed positions. There were at least forty small black beads, a dozen larger white beads, and one or two each of larger green, red and yellow beads. "The planets," he said. "You've seen something like this?"

"Not like that," Covington said. "Do the planets go around in circles?" He could not think of another way to say "orbit". He made circular motions with his hands, trying to illustrate.

Card looked puzzled. "They spin on their axes," he said, and twirled a bead on its wire by way of illustration.

"No, I mean do they circle around each other?"

"How could a planet do that?" Card asked. "Sometimes they move a little this way or that way, but they always come back to their position."

"Which one is Brythe?" Wiegand asked. Card pointed to a green-painted bead, one of two in the frame. Then he pointed to a white bead and said "This is Home."

"There are — what? — twelve white beads like Home," Covington said. "Are they all human worlds?" Card nodded. "Then why is Brythe a different color and size?"

"Brythe is as big as Cortay Planet, although it has a human ecology," Card said. "It's heavier than the other human worlds. In fact, it's the only human world that is not the same size."

"How about all those little black things?" Wiegand asked.

"Those are size one worlds, little and with no air. Very useless," Card said. "Sometimes the Cortays mine minerals on them. Otherwise no one goes there."

"Size one?"

"We call that size 'one'," Card explained. "Then the human worlds are size 12, Cortay Planet and Brythe are 14s. The red ones are size 16, we don't go there much, and the one yellow one is the world of the Hands of God, which is size 32."

"1, 12, 14, 16, 32," said Covington in a dull voice. "Bingo. The light dawns."

"What have you got?" Wiegand asked.

Covington sat motionless for a long moment. Finally he roused himself and pointed to the wooden balls. "Hydrogen, carbon, nitrogen, oxygen, sulfur," he said in English. "Atomic weight 1, 12, 14, 16, 32. We're living on an atomic nucleus. Dear Lord, it all comes together. The arches in the sky are electron orbitals, the light is force-carrier photons that the nucleus exchanges with the electrons. Somehow we were shrunk down super small and we're inside in a molecule. How's that grab you?"

"It's insane," Wiegand said promptly. "But that's not to say I'm disagreeing with you. I sure as hell don't have any better ideas."

"Talk to me, fellows," Card said. "I don't understand what you're saying."

Covington stood and began pacing back and forth, still sipping his tea. "Card," he said.

"Gron Orrata Hemmet Card."

"Yeah, whatever. Can you draw me the symbol for water?"

"Sure." There were sliding blackboards in front of shelves on one wall. Card retrieved a stick of what seemed to be white soap and drew with it. He drew two little boxes which fit together along one jagged edge like puzzle pieces. Each box had a letter in it.

"There you go," Covington said. "There's no way in hell any kind of Earth chemistry would represent aitch-two-oh that way. This isn't water."

"We've been drinking it, mopping with it and washing dishes in it for weeks," Wiegand said.

"Still. It's not just that it's not water, it's not even atoms and molecules the way we understand them. We're *inside* a molecule."

Card looked from one to the other as they talked in English. "So atomic nuclei are covered with smaller atoms, sort of a crust? " Wiegand asked. "Why wouldn't we have known that, back in reality-land?"

"Well, if you were studying planets in our solar system by whacking them with other planets to see what pieces come out," Covington said, "I don't think you'd notice the atmosphere or oceans. That's pretty much how we study the structure of atoms. Air, water and people are really just a tiny fraction of the mass of the Earth. I don't think it's impossible or even particularly unreasonable to think that the properties of atomic particles are emergent effects from the interaction of lots of smaller parts."

He blinked, sat down and laughed. "Man, if I ever got back home I could write a killer paper on this. I'll call them 'Covington's Itty Bitty Atoms.' Copyright, trademark, all rights reserved, not to be re-used without permission of Major League Baseball."

"If you got home," Wiegand said, "I don't think there's a way in hell you could demonstrate the existence of little-bitty atoms. CERN and Fermilab together couldn't whack an atom hard enough to bring that out."

"Yeah. We're not going home anyway," Covington said miserably, slumping on the stool Wiegand put a hand on his shoulder.

"Guys," Card said, "talk to me in regular language. Talk to me now."

"What time are services at the church?" Covington abruptly demanded. Card pulled down a stop-clock, started it and pointed to a mark that seemed to be about an hour away.

"Okay, pal. Got another one of whatever you've been drinking? Let me tell you a story before I go off to church," Covington said.

Card had beer, in a refrigerator under the counter which also held biological samples. He pulled out a bottle and poured it into the tea cups.

They sat down together at the lab bench. Covington and Wiegand told Card their story from the beginning.

Chapter 9

The downtown church was beginning to fill up. "How does everybody know what time the service is if nobody has a clock?" Covington asked Card.

He shrugged. "It's the right time for the service," he said. "If you don't know that, I don't know how else to explain it. We should get inside if you want to get a seat. This priest talks a long time. You don't want to stand up at the back."

"Brian," Wiegand said, "you go ahead. Personally, I don't need any more weirdness for a while, and I can't stand the thought of being surrounded by people right now. I'm going to go for a walk and maybe go beat my head against a wall until the voices quiet down, you know? I'll meet you back at the restaurant."

"You going to be okay?" Covington asked.

"Sure, sure. This town doesn't seem dangerous. I'm not *really* going to hit my head, doofus."

"Okay. You understand going to church is something I kind of have to do?"

"No problem. Gron Orrata Hemmet Card, thanks for all your help. I'm sorry we went crazy on you there."

"I'm still trying to understand this," Card said. "We'll talk again, all right?"

"We will. Okay, see you later."

"Flow with it," Card said. He and Covington entered the church hall.

The clouds overhead were breaking up, letting through a warm autumnal light. Wiegand drifted off down a side street, wondering how the natives described directions without the sun as a reference. He could see fragments of the arches in the sky — electron orbitals, dripping photons down to the ground and catching the photons that streamed up from mountains, roof peaks of houses, tips of leaves and pointed lamps. In the display window of a grocer's shop, he could see vegetables arranged in neat rows, odd-shaped but not really any stranger than vegetables he had seen in Mexican supermarkets in Chicago. A family passed him on the way to church, with a little girl dressed up in sparkling white trousers, shirt and wide-brimmed white hat. Her hair, including the hair down her back, was tied with colored ribbon bows. She smiled at him as she passed, and he smiled back.

Every atom a world! Hydrogen nuclei were airless asteroids, and oxygen and sulfur nuclei were gas giants, too heavy for humans. Humans lived, or could live, on carbon and nitrogen nuclei.

An unthinkable number of worlds, even if you just considered the atoms in the air between your two hands, back on Earth. Millions of trillions — there were no meaningful words for such a number.

Suppose that he and Covington had been reincarnated, for whatever reason, on the nucleus-world most like Earth within the space where they had vanished. The lab that had held the Dense Memory Device had benches and chairs, their own bodies and all the apparatus he and Covington had installed. There were more than enough atoms within a few feet to meet the preposterously unlikely odds of finding a separate evolution that resulted in human beings. *Star Trek* aliens indeed!

It occurred to him that from the point of view of his old body, he had been re-created, more or less, on a tiny scale in a location nearby. But from the point of view of his new body, re-making his body on Earth would mean arranging the motions of an unthinkable number of "stars" and "galaxies" in the sky above him.

Which meant that he was never going home to Earth, never, never, never. He closed his eyes and turned his face up to the bright "sun" light, standing motionless on the sidewalk. The light felt like sunlight, the air was air, the sounds around him sounded like a small town. He breathed deeply, opened his eyes and after a long interval started walking again.

The center of New Town was on a slight rise of ground, sloping down gently to the river that curved through the flat farmland. The street Wiegand was on passed through a shabby district of tiny houses, used-clothing stores, bars, a used-book store, various odds-and-ends shops. It led down to a brick bridge over the river. There was also a small church in the soggy, cheap land near the river. A few latecomers were straggling in through the door of the church as Wiegand passed by. He wondered, looking at it, if the priest there held communion for his flock directly in the real river.

On the other side of the river was the spaceport.

He stood on the bridge, lost in thought for a while, looking down at the clear flowing "water" edged with reeds and leafy plants, then gazing out over the spaceport. Once a truck came past the guardhouse and through the gate in the chain-link fence around the spaceport. He stood to one side for it as it rumbled over the bridge, then went back to musing. A fish jumped in the river.

The spaceport was a flat expanse of grassy lawn divided by access roads, ringed by wooden warehouses and workshops. There was one spaceship in port, as tall as a three-story building and wide enough to fill the space between two access roads. The dome of the hamburger-bun shape was painted green with elaborate white filigree lines, and the base was dark yellow. There were cargo doors and hatches all around the base, and a crew of humans at one door loading goods manually from a truck.

He was close enough to see that the ship was extensively decorated. There were painted garlands and ribbons around the doors, rows of colored glass lights that did not seem to have any utilitarian purpose, and even painted panels that seemed to be advertising. It looked like a carnival tent.

A few buildings crowded outside the fence between the spaceport and the river. One of them had a sign with a glass of beer painted on it, and presently Wiegand walked inside.

The interior was plain white-painted wood. There were benches inside and chairs with a few men lounging in them. Near the back wall, seated on a heavier chair, was a Cortay.

It was taller than a man, and a yard or more wide across the shoulders. The blue-furred body had no head. Instead, there was an eye near each shoulder, and a speaking mouth and various smaller orifices in the chest. The two legs were skinny, covered with darker fur that shaded into black. It wore shorts and boots, and was drinking a glass of beer.

Since the Cortay didn't seem to bother anyone else, Wiegand ignored it and took a seat at an empty bench. The fat bartender came out and he ordered a beer, holding out two pennies with resignation. The bartender tucked one penny in his apron and gave the other back. "Haven't seen you before," he said. "You usually drink in town, eh?"

"Not so much," Wiegand said. "It's only one ... one coin, here?"

"Here, and every place that isn't some kind of [something] hall," the bartender said. He went to his barrel and returned with a glass.

Wiegand repeated the unknown word and asked, "What does that mean?"

The bartender laughed and demonstrated dancing, skipping a sarcastic step left and right. "Dancing boys bring their girlfriends there," he said. "We don't do that here."

"Okay," Wiegand said, grinning. He hoisted his glass toward the other. "Here's to some serious drinking, no dancing."

Behind him, the Cortay said in a low, rumbling voice, "New fellow. Come and talk to me, please." Wiegand turned, and the Cortay waved to him amiably.

He stood and moved to the alien's table. "Glad to," Wiegand said. "How is it that you speak my language?"

The Cortay regarded him with its widely-spaced eyes. It had a strong but not unpleasant smell, something like motor oil. "I don't speak your language," it said. "You speak my language, except that I think you are just learning it."

"I ..." Wiegand realized he could not phrase what he was thinking. "I didn't know that," he said lamely.

"Then you are from a planet outside of our space," the Cortay said. "Very interesting. Please tell me what planet you are from."

"Earth," Wiegand said helplessly. "It's kind of a complicated story."

"It must be. I have not heard of your planet."

"How did you know I was from a different planet?"

"Your smell, which is distinctive," the Cortay said, taking a drink of beer. "Also, your body posture tells me you are tense, meeting me, although there is no need to be. Also, you were going to pay the downtown price for your beer."

"Busted," Wiegand said helplessly, using the English word. He continued in what he supposed was the Cortay language, "What are you going to do with me now?"

"Nothing. Fear nothing," the Cortay said. If it had a smile, or any body language, it was not apparent. "But we have long thought there was another human empire in space, or more than one. Assuming you come from there, I could become very rich by representing you to my people. But I will wait and let you make up your own mind about that."

"Arghh," Wiegand muttered, and drank from his beer. "Let me ask a dumb human question. Are you male or female?"

"I am male."

"Hiya, pal. My name's Pete Wiegand."

"I am Oktorum. Is 'Pete' a place or an organization?"

"Neither one, it's just me. You can call me 'Sad For Pete', I suppose. Don't you have an attachment to your name?"

"That is not the custom among Cortays."

"Okay, Oktorum. So tell me. Why do humans speak your language?"

"We are the only space-faring race, at least in this part of the universe. When we discovered your planet Home, about 100,000 days ago, you were savages living in caves and hollow trees. Since then, guided by the Hands of God, we have given you our language, taught you and brought you up to develop civilization."

On Wiegand's urgent request, the bartender found a pad of brewery order forms and a pencil. Wiegand began figuring on the blank side of a sheet of paper. "A 'day' is the time between two sleeps, right? Assuming that averages out to about the same as a regular day, then 100,000 days is ... about two hundred seventy years? Are you seriously telling me human civilization is only two or three hundred years old?"

"Tell me what a 'year' is."

"365 days."

"Interesting! Now why would you make a unit of time for that peculiar number of days?"

"Oh ... that's complicated too. Anyway, 100,000 days ago you first landed on Home and the humans were savages?"

"Exactly," the Cortay said. "This is schoolboy knowledge, for everybody but you. The Hands of God helped us to understand you, and then required that we help you grow into a civilized people."

"You work for them?"

The Cortay sighed, a very human sound. "It amounts to that. The Hands are so intelligent, they can make use of our own laws and customs better even than we can ourselves. We discovered them on their planet only about 20,000 days before we found you, and by the time we found your planet, the Hands of God were already in charge of anything they wanted to control."

"How do you mean?" Wiegand asked. With a great deal of sketching, hand-waving and discussion, he and the Cortay were eventually able to get across the words for "patents" and "stock" and "inventions," and it became clear after a while that the Hands never left their own planet but had managed to work themselves into positions of control in Cortay society based on nothing but irresistible intelligence.

"What do you think I can do for you?" Wiegand finally asked.

"If your planet has products to trade," Oktorum said, "I could set up a trading company that is not controlled by the Hands — at least, not at first — and become very rich trading with you."

"I sure wish I could help you," Wiegand said. "But I can't contact my planet. I haven't got a thing to offer."

"Can you explain more?"

"I really can't. At least, not now," Wiegand said, and changed the subject. "So civilization on this planet is less than three hundred years old?"

"No, no, the civilization on *Home* is three hundred 'years' old. Brythe wasn't settled until about 10,000 days ago."

"Thirty years," Wiegand said, after more arithmetic. "Yeah, that seems about right. I guess that's when they built 'New Town'. Why did they come to Brythe?"

"There are minerals that are plentiful only here and on my planet, and my planet is thickly settled and hard to mine. Also, they can build factories cheaply here and nobody cares if the factory dumps garbage in the river as long as it's on the side that flows away from the city," the Cortay said.

Some of the other men in the bar had been listening, and now a couple of them came forward to join the conversation. "Flow with it," one man said, a graying middle-aged man who was very strongly built even for a Brythean, "my name's Sad For Arkum. I load ships. I've been here since the beginning. I was in the third ship that came here from Home."

Wiegand introduced himself, and the Cortay introduced himself as "Oktorum. I am the navigator on the *Passenger and Cargo Craft Type 8 No. 215*."

"That's the only ship that's in port right now," Arkum said to Wiegand. "Anyway, I left a good job on Home to come here because they said we'd all get rich. They have ore here! They have rare minerals! We'll build factories and farms! Everybody makes money!"

"I take it it didn't work out that way?" Wiegand asked, grinning.

"Some guys got rich, mainly the ones who were rich to begin with. Not me."

Another man said, "They didn't exactly *cheat* us, but most of us haven't made enough money to afford to go back to Home permanently, either."

"So this planet was empty before you got here?" Wiegand asked.

"Sure was," Arkum said. "Up until they found out you could get minerals here, this was the most useless place you ever heard of. I think it's too heavy for humans, although the kids are used to it — I mean, I'm still beat at the end of every day and I've been here most of my life, now. But the Cortays don't like it because it smells like a human world."

Wiegand looked at Oktorum, who blinked his eyes slowly. "I would not criticize someone else's planet," he said. "This is your home, not mine. It's true that the weight here is right for my kind, but we don't like to stay here because it has an ecology like one of the human worlds. We can breathe the air here but it smells odd to us."

"How many people live on this planet?" Wiegand asked.

"Only about 20,000," Arkum said. "That's one of the reasons we noticed you. It's kind of a small town, and I sort of know most of the faces around here."

"I guess I do have that out-of-towner look."

"Also, you know, that hat," Arkum said.

"I'm going back as soon as I can get the money together," one of the men said. "I don't like it here anymore, with all the earthquakes we've been getting." A number of others nodded agreement to that.

"Oktorum," Arkum said, "do you know if the earthquakes are just around here, or do they also have them at Rendellis Port?"

"They're all over the planet, and becoming more frequent," Oktorum said. "As far as I know, nobody knows why. We've got orders to get the ship off the ground if it happens again while we're here. The Hands of God say they're studying it."

"I'm Sad For Ulmatter," another man said. "As long as the Hands are on it, I'll stick around. They can find a solution if there is one."

"Yeah, I don't mean I don't trust the Hands," the other said. "I'm just, you know, nervous about it."

"What do the Hands of God do for you?" Wiegand asked.

"You talk to them and they tell you what to do," Ulmatter said. "Why don't you know that?"

"Um, I forget things," Wiegand said warily.

"The Hands can tell the druggist — well, maybe not here, but on Home — they can tell the druggist what to mix for a memory problem," Arkum said. "If you really need some kind of drug, they'll have somebody mix it and ship it to you here. When I was having trouble with my wife a couple of years ago, they gave me some pills and told me exactly what I needed to know about myself and about her, and we patched it up. You won't catch *me* doubting the Hands."

"When I was depressed and drinking too much, they got my head straight," another man said.

"They got me a better job and helped me get out of debt," another said.

"We have known the Hands of God for longer than your civilization," Oktorum said, "and they have always been good for us. Everything they do leads to the best for my race, and when they tell us to do something for your race, it's always best for you."

"Okay, okay, I get it. I didn't mean to step on anybody's toes," Wiegand said. "I'm just asking, I'm sure they're nice folks. How do you get in touch with these Hands?"

"You ask the priest, and if he thinks it's all right, he lets you into the room in the church where you talk to them," Arkum said. "Even if the priest doesn't want to let you in, there are a couple of other places you can go."

"Pay no attention to the man behind the curtain," Wiegand muttered in English, then added in Cortay, "I guess I should go talk to the Hands of God."

"Do that," Oktorum said. "But then come back and talk to me, about what we discussed. I can help you, and we can both profit from it."

"I'm not going to be as helpful as I think you think I'll be," Wiegand said. "But I know another guy who might want to talk to you."

"My ship will be here for at least three more days," Oktorum said.

There was a rumble coming up through the floor of the bar. The men turned to watch a truck going by outside. One of them laughed weakly and said, "It's a truck. For a moment there, I thought it was ..."

The ground continued to rumble. "It *is* an earthquake," another yelled. "I just saw that truck slip sideways." They ran outside in a panic, the Cortay with them.

By the time they reached the street the temblor was over, with no damage and not even an extra cloud of dust. Wiegand thought about standing by the railroad tracks when he was a kid, feeling the rumbling of the huge strings of coal cars heading for the steel mills.

He stopped, struck by the ideas of coal and of something moving underground below him. "Oktorum," he said, "is the sky different here than on your planet?"

"How do you mean?"

"A different set of ... of those things," Wiegand said, pointing to the arches in the sky.

"The orbitals?" the Cortay said, giving him the local word. "Yes, they're different on my planet. This place is more like the other human worlds."

Wiegand stood stock-still for a moment, then said, "I've gotta go." He began running over the bridge back to town.

"Come on back," Arkum yelled. "It's okay, it was just a little shake!"

Wiegand waved back at him but kept running, heading toward the church where he had left Covington.

He knew, now, what Brythe was.

Chapter 10

There was not a single element in the church service that struck Covington as unearthly. Inevitably he made comparisons: this ritual was like his church at home, that was more Catholic, this was like a New Age sort of ceremony he had attended at the behest of a girl he liked in college, that vaguely suggested a picture in *National Geographic* of some Asiatic temple.

None of it was working for him.

He hunched down in his wooden pew, looking around at the sea of hats, up at the decorated ceiling, down at his hands. The old priest at the altar led a call-and-response Covington could not understand, did complicated things with wood and metal instruments and spoke part of the time in rhyme. He was clearly more of a "priest" than a "minister," and Covington was beginning to dislike him. When he started his sermon, Covington caught about every third word.

Card, sitting beside him, was no help at all. "He sure does go on," is all Card would whisper.

Covington did catch that the priest mentioned the "Hands of God" a dozen times.

When they brought out the river troughs, Covington stood with the rest. This church was big enough to have six troughs in use at one time, all of them crafted nicely of golden polished wood with contrasting inlays. Both men and women stood together at the same trough here (big city liberals, he thought). He understood the symbolism of the cold water flowing across his hand, but felt as isolated and lonely as before.

The young woman who dipped her hand in the trough across from him caught his eye. She was beautiful, with thick, soft black hair cut shoulder-length under a pretty wide-brimmed hat. She was dressed in what he was coming to recognize as a fashionable style, with a tan jacket over her white shirt and loose tan trousers with a contrasting red seam on the outside. She wore black pumps with slightly high heels.

She glanced at his hat and smiled.

Covington spent a few annoyed minutes, while the priest spoke again, looking at the hats worn by the other men. This seemed to be a fairly upscale church — the younger men looked like middle-manager types rather than working men. They wore a variety of hats, and as far as he could tell, his hat wasn't much different from some of theirs. But obviously, there was some fashion cue he was missing.

Eventually they passed the collection basket, a part of the service that was stunningly familiar. Covington examined his stash of eighteen small coins and put in four of them. Paper money did not seem to be in use in New Town, but most of the other coins in the basket were larger than his. The congregation sang another hymn and, after a little more ritual, were done. It came as a relief.

A minute or two after the end of the service, the ground began to shake. Everyone ran headlong into the street, parents clutching their children, and the building was empty in a moment. By the time they reached the outside, the shaking was over. There was no damage, no more movement, nothing to see or worry about. The panic turned back on itself and became laughter.

It was suddenly a festival, a church social, a street party! A few young couples started a spontaneous dance to work off their nervous energy, and the children erupted into a wild game of tag in and through the crowd. The priest sent a few men back into the church building to bring out the refreshments that had been set up in the common room. They brought out folding tables and set up urns of tea and plates of sweetmeats. After ten minutes, no one could have known that the outdoor gathering was not a long-planned event.

Card and Covington took cups of tea and stood to one side. The young woman Covington had noticed came up to introduce herself. "Hi," she said. "I'm Church Sani. Welcome!" She was fresh and even prettier in the outside light.

"Sad For Brian Covington," Covington said. "I'm new here. Does your name mean your group is the church?"

"It does," she said, and favored him with a blinding smile. "Of course, everyone is part of the church, but for me, it's my primary association."

"Gron Orrata Hemmet Card," Card said. He bowed to her.

"Gron Orrata!" Sani said, beaming. "I went there too! Not 'Hemmet', I was in the business school. How nice to meet you here!"

"'Hemmet'?" Covington asked.

"It's the name of the science school," Card said. "Church Sani, here, must have been over on the other end of campus. You're an administrator?"

"I'm an accountant," she said. "I'm here doing audits of local churches for the head church on Home."

"Is there a problem?" Card asked.

"Not at all. Just routine. I'll only be here for half-a-thousand days or so, then I'll go back home. Once I get back to Home and normal gravity I'll be the strongest accountant on the planet." She favored them with another hundred-watt smile. "Is there a Gron Orrata alumni group here? Is that your association?" she asked.

"No," Card said sourly. "All the Gron Orrata people I know of are in better-paying jobs on Home."

"Oh. You must have really loved that school if your affiliation is with a group that isn't even on this planet."

"I did. I do," Card said. "I'm not connected to Brythe any more than I can help."

If Sani was embarrassed at provoking this personal admission, it did not dim her perkiness a bit. She turned to Covington and said, "I can tell that you're new here."

"The hat, right?" Covington sighed.

"The hat, and now that you speak, your accent. What planet are you from?"

"Earth," he said hesitantly, and waited.

"I haven't heard of that one," she said. "What brings you here?"

"I don't quite know how to answer that," Covington said.

Card said. "I think the Hands might like to meet Sad For Brian Covington. We should go talk to the priest."

"That would be a new one," Sani said. "I've met a lot of people who wanted to talk to the Hands of God, but I can't say I ever met anybody who thought the Hands should want to talk to him. Sad For Brian Covington, your friend must think you're pretty special."

"Call me Sad For Brian," Covington said.

"Okay. But then what's the 'Covington' part?"

"That's hard to explain, too," Covington said desperately. "But anyway, could I talk to the priest? Could you introduce me or something? I need to go to the priest to be able to talk to the Hands, right?"

"You do," Sani said. "Sure, I can introduce you, or anybody can. But look, is there anything I can do to help, myself? We're all here to help each other."

Covington thought for a long moment. "If I talk to the priest, will he tell anybody else what I said?" he finally asked.

"Oh, no. And you don't have to tell the priest everything, anyway. Just enough to convince him to let you talk to the Hands. The Hands always want all the details. But Sad For Brian, where *are* you from that you don't know that?"

Card jumped back in. "Church Sani, we'd better let him explain it direct to the Hands."

"Certainly. I don't mean to pry. I'll bring you over to God Nanhallit as soon as he's through talking with that lady there."

Covington winced. "The priest is named 'God'?" he asked.

"The priest is not *named* 'God', silly," Sani said with asperity. "His association is with God."

Card stepped back, sensing a developing argument. "So your association is with the church," Covington said, "and the priest is connected directly to God. You're not connected directly to God yourself?"

"I'm not a priest," she said. "Of course I talk to God, I've been part of the church all my life. But why would we want anybody to be a priest whose primary connection is not God? Sad For Brian, you ask the *oddest* questions."

"I'm a long way from home," Covington muttered. "Yeah, please, let me talk to the God guy."

"I think you've got another visitor first," Sani said. She pointed over Covington's shoulder, and he turned to see Wiegand running up the road toward him, puffing and gasping.

"Brian! Gotta talk to you!" he yelled in English before he stopped. Card thoughtfully brought over one of the folding chairs that had been brought out, and Wiegand collapsed into it, unable to talk any further.

"I'll talk to you again. Flow with it," Sani said, and moved away to socialize with another acquaintance in the crowd.

Wiegand was still gasping but spoke to Card. "Card, I don't want to be mysterious but can I talk to Brian in my own language for a few minutes? Kind of important."

"Sure, sure," Card said. "I'm going to go back to my lab anyway. I need something better than church tea, you know what I mean? But I'll talk to you tomorrow after lunch, I don't have a class then." They waved to him as he walked off.

"Here's some water, slow down. You need to go away from here?" Covington asked.

"Not as long as we're speaking English, I guess. Brian, I met a Cortay down at the spaceport and talked to him. Brythe is not a nitrogen atom. I mean nucleus."

"Eh? It's a 14. What is it, then?"

"It's *carbon-14*. Same size, different charge, different number of electrons."

Covington said. "Carbon-14 is unstable. You think it's gonna ... "

"It's going to explode, or whatever carbon-14 does," Wiegand said. "I think that's what the earthquakes are about. It's getting ready to have a whatchamacallit."

"Beta decay," Covington said absently. "I need to think about that." He had a pencil from the restaurant, and looked around to find a stack of paper flyers advertising some church event or other one of the tables. He quickly took a couple of sheets, and he and Wiegand dragged chairs over to an unused corner of a table. They hunched over the paper.

"Beta decay isn't that big of deal, I don't think. If this planet is a carbon-14, it'll throw off an electron and I think some kind of neutrino, and turn into nitrogen-14. Neutrinos are practically nothing and an electron isn't very big. I don't think that's enough to blame earthquakes on."

"You know more than I do," Wiegand said. "You're the chemist."

"Materials scientist," Covington said. "I'm pretty good on nano-scale thermal transfer structures in copper. Nuclear physics, not so much."

"Well, I read a magazine article on carbon-14 dating," Wiegand said. "That's my contribution."

"All right, hold your water," Covington said. "An electron has mass, just not very much. It's 1/1836th the mass of a proton, that I do remember. Carbon-14 has six protons and eight neutrons, for a total of 14 atomic masses, give or take. So an electron would be 1/1836th of 1/14th of whatever mass this planet is."

He scratched with the pencil, muttering "So here's the world-famous scientist suddenly realizing that his brain has gotten as soft as Cheez-Whiz from years of working on computers, and he can just barely do arithmetic by hand any more. Let's say that Brythe is the same size as the Earth. Earth is about 4000 miles in radius, so that gives it a volume of four-thirds pi r-cubed which is ... holy crap, 2.6 trillion cubic miles? Man, the numbers go up fast when you get cubes in there.

"So that divided by 14, divided by 1836, comes to ... ". Covington stopped and stared at his figures. He mutter, "Oh, my God. My God."

"What have you got, Brian?" Wiegand asked.

Covington swallowed. "I'm assuming whatever kind of mass an electron is made of, it's pretty much the same as whatever kind of mass this planet is made of — rocks and dirt, you know?" he said. "That means if this place is the same relative size as Earth, an electron would be something like *ten million cubic miles* of matter."

"How big is that around?"

"Give me a minute. I can't do cube roots by hand, I'll have to try some numbers and estimate." Covington wrote furiously, then said, "You know how big an electron would be? If it's a sphere, it's something like 250 miles in diameter."

Wiegand said slowly, "It's exploding out instead of falling in, but I don't suppose that will help a bit. This is going to be exactly like getting hit with an asteroid 250 miles wide. That's bigger than the asteroid that took out the dinosaurs."

"A lot bigger," Covington said dully, and bent his head to pray.

Wiegand shook him on the shoulder angrily. "Hold off a minute on the praying," he said. "Talk to *me*, I'm right here. Blowing off a chunk of rock, or something, that size is going to be like an asteroid strike or an atomic war, am I right?"

"It'll be everything an atomic war would be, and a lot worse," Covington said. "This planet is going to ring like a barrelhouse banjo. It'll crack the crust and start volcanoes erupting, assuming they have volcanoes. It will raise so much dust and smoke there'll be a nuclear winter for, I don't know, years. Earthquakes, tsunamis, mudslides, either melting or expanding the polar ice caps if they have those." He looked up at Wiegand. "Everybody dies. Everybody, every single one."

"Okay, let's get a grip," Wiegand said. "Turns out — this is something else I just learned — it turns out there's only about twenty thousand people on this planet. That would be doable, to evacuate that many. They have spaceships and they have someplace else these people could go to. If we can convince somebody to order an evacuation, we could get through this."

"Yeah," Covington said thoughtfully. "Yeah, there's a way out, maybe. Look, I'm going to go back into the sanctuary to pray, and if you get in my way I'll knock you down, you understand me?"

"Okay, Brian," Wiegand said. "Leave me the pencil, will you?"

Covington walked slowly back into the church sanctuary. The big room was empty and his footsteps echoed from the brick floor as he made his way up the center aisle and sat down at the end of a pew. He bent his head and prayed silently.

After quite a long time, he became aware that there was another person on the pew near him. Covington looked up and saw Sani sitting a little distance away. She was also praying, but she looked up when he did.

"Sad For Brian," she said. "May I pray with you? Sometimes that helps."

"Thanks," he said ungraciously. "But you couldn't possibly have any idea what I'm going through, here."

"Do you think I haven't had sorrow in my life?" she asked. "You don't know me."

"Nobody's had something like this to deal with," Covington said.

"I told the priest you wanted to talk to him. He's waiting in his office, if you still want to go. Or you can talk to me, or not."

"Hell, I'll talk to all of you. Let's get Pete back and make it group therapy, why not? You'll all find out sooner or later anyway." Covington stood and walked abruptly toward the door. He said over his shoulder, "Wait here, I'll be back with Pete. You do some uninterrupted prayer in the meantime. Somebody ought to."

He brought Wiegand back inside and said "Church Sani, this is my friend Sad For Pete. Pete, this is Church Sani. " In an aside, in English, he said, "You know, like in 'Sani-Flush,' not that you should ever say that or think it again."

"Oh, great," Wiegand muttered. "Now I'll never get that out of my head."

Sani flashed a tentative smile at Wiegand and led them to a side room where God Nanhallit was sitting, doing paperwork. She introduced them all around.

"Church Sani tells me you need to see me," the priest said. He was a thin old man. His hair was still thick but white, including the hair down his back. He had changed from the hat he wore during the service into a small round cap like a yarmulke. "I'll be glad to talk to you, and if I can't help you, I can let you talk to the Hands. Sani, would you leave us now?"

"Please, let her stay," Covington said. "This affects her too, and everybody, and I could use another opinion anyway."

"Is there some immediate danger?" the priest asked. "Do I need to warn people about something?"

Covington hesitated, and Wiegand jumped in. "We don't know," he said. "We know about a disaster that's going to happen, but we don't have any idea how long or how short a time we have."

"Then let's not panic," Nanhallit said, sitting back and folding his hands. "There's tea in the pot over there. Get some, and then tell us what you want to tell us."

"Okay," Covington said, sighing. "This will be the second time I've told this tale today. If I tell it enough, I'll get pretty good at this. Are you familiar with the village of Dogat?"

He and Wiegand told their story again, holding back nothing, explaining everything at length.

Nanhallit watched their faces impassively, and Sani became visibly more anxious as they spoke.

"So that's what we know," Wiegand finally finished. "We don't know how we got here or why, if there is a why, but if we're right about the electron expulsion, unless we can get enough spaceships here to evacuate everybody, every person on Brythe is going to die. We told this to Gron Orrata Hemmet Card this morning, except for the explosion part, and he believed us. Do you believe us?"

"No," the priest said.

God Nanhallit continued, "I cannot lie and I will not patronize you. I don't believe your story, although I'm sure that something traumatic did happen to you both."

"(Now that I think about it)," Wiegand whispered to Covington in English, "(there's a joke. 'You want help? Talk to the Hand!')". Covington grinned sourly.

"*Can* we talk to the Hands of God?" he asked aloud. "They're supposed to be really smart."

The priest grinned. "In this job, I have learned to handle insults," he said genially. "Sad For Brian, please consider for a moment that you may be wrong. You *are* wrong. One of the commonest mental distortions is to imagine yourself to be a man of power and influence, and then to rationalize why you find yourself in humble circumstances. I've counseled men who believed they were rich, and that enemies had stolen their money. I counseled a woman once who was convinced she was a queen, and she had some reason (I forget what it was) for why she was working as a store clerk.

"Now you've come to me with the story of how you used to be important, and I must say you've topped anybody else I ever heard of. You were vaster than the sky, bigger than all the worlds combined, bigger than the Universe ... and then somehow you were shrunk and thrown into the mud and had to work as a dishwasher. Your friend Sad For Pete corroborates your story and the two of you encourage each other to develop it in even more detail.

"Do you see that absolutely everything that happens now, such as earthquakes, will turn out to be evidence for your story as long as you keep weaving it into your narrative?

"Sad For Brian, Sad For Pete, you don't need to talk to the Hands. You need to talk to *me*, and you need to ask God for help and accept it when He gives it. Will you let me give you that help?"

Wiegand began to cloud up with anger, but Covington waved at him to sit back down. "God Nanhallit," he said, standing, "thank you for listening to us. I can't find any fault with what you're saying, and truthfully, if you had come to *me* with a story like mine, I'd figure you were crazy too. But I've been hanging around church folk for so long I think I can pick out the real goofballs, and I don't think I'm one of them. Also, I've trusted God for guidance all my life, and I think he's still holding me in his hands. I'm not wrong about this."

"You have prayed to God and He has told you all this?" the priest asked.

"Oh, no," Covington said, smiling. "God never tells me stuff like that. The only thing God ever tells me is that He loves me." He turned to go.

Wiegand looked at Church Sani. "Do *you* think we're insane?" he asked. "Because to tell you the God's truth, I'm not so sure we're not. Or at least, I'm not so sure I'm not. It's sure a crazy story."

"I don't know what to think," she said hesitantly. "I think I need to talk to the Hands."

"We both do," Nanhallit said. "Not together, they don't usually do that. But I feel the need for some advice, myself."

"You do that," Covington said. "Pete and I, we're going to wash dishes."

"Your turn to wash," Wiegand said. "I'm drying."

* * *

On the way out of the church, they met Vallow coming toward them.

"Let me guess," Wiegand said. "You're coming here because you need to talk to a priest in order to talk to the Hands of God. Right?"

"That is right," Vallow said. "You also?"

"Us also, and you're wasting your time. Or at least, the priest didn't believe us and we don't get to talk to the Hands, whoever they are."

"You also are just learning the language," Vallow said. "I thought you might have a story like mine."

"Oh, we've got a story," Covington said. "I have two questions. I assume you got to this planet in a spaceship of some kind. Does your planet, wherever it is, have more ships?"

"Certainly," Vallow said. "I came alone, and was wrecked, but I come from a [something] of twenty

119

planets, quite far from here, and there are many ships. What was your other question?"

"The second question is, you got any money? We know a bar that has cheap beer. Let's go drink beer and tell stories."

"I have some money," Vallow said, "I need help and I'd like to talk to you. As far as the beer, I'll drink it for the sake of friendship. But if I ever get in touch with my home world, I'm going to get rich selling decent beer to this group of worlds."

"Shipping is cheap enough that you could make money importing beer?"

"Yes."

"*You*, my friend, are exactly the man we need to talk to. Let's go."

Chapter 11

His federation, Vallow said, comprised twenty human planets, all size 12, which Covington and Wiegand understood to be carbon nuclei. They also had some heavier worlds — nitrogens and oxygens — inhabited by non-human races who were friendly or indifferent, but not part of the federation. They did not have Cortays or the Hands of God. They had very occasional contact with other empires living still farther away from the Home space.

"I am not a representative of my government, or of anybody," Vallow over his second beer, in the bar by the spaceport. "I came this way trying to establish some trade, but I wrecked my ship. I made it to a farm village and they sent me to New Town, and here I am.

If I can build or find a communicator, I can contact my people and someone will come for me."

Oktorum, the Cortay, had not been in the bar when they arrived but one of the men who worked at the port had volunteered to fetch him. Now he leaned forward, his huge shoulders as broad as the table at which they sat, and regarded Vallow with his wide-spaced eyes. "Probably the communicator on my ship can be adapted to the frequencies your people use," he said.

"I'd be very grateful if you can help me," Vallow said.

"I would like to import products from your worlds to ours. I think there's profit there."

"I'm sure there is, and I could sure use a Cortay partner. I'm thinking of starting with this beer, which tastes like it was brewed through a [something]."

"I thought humans liked this beer," Oktorum said. "It is made from a Cortay recipe. Very delicious."

"*That* explains the taste," Vallow said. "Listen, we have human recipes for beer which will sell better, at least to humans. Trust me on this point."

"I also hope we will be able to deal in technical products for which the Hands do not hold all the patents," Oktorum added. "The Hands are good, but we would like to have things that don't belong to them."

"Well, I think our culture is ahead of the humans here, but not much if any ahead of yours, technically," Vallow said. "But I'm sure we can find something to get rich on. I have one other story to add. About 150,000 days ago, another planet in our group sent out a ship of colonists to find a new, empty world, for what I think were religious reasons. They were never heard from again. I'm wondering if the people of Home are their descendants."

"That makes sense," Covington said. "Those bones-on-the-outside horses they use don't have any common ancestors with humans."

"We've always had the theory that humans evolved on one planet and then spread out," Vallow said. "No one has ever agreed on what planet that might have been. Now tell us about your home world."

"Okay, yeah," Wiegand said, then hesitated for a long moment. "Look, we bought you beers, right? We shared our water and leftovers, right? So you have to be nice and listen to us. It's a long story."

"That is also the custom on our worlds," Vallow said graciously. "But I would give you a respectful hearing in any case. So say on."

"I will listen," Oktorum said.

"Well, here's the whole dog-and-pony show," Wiegand said, and they launched into their story again from the beginning.

" ... and that's what we think these earthquakes are leading up to," Covington finished the tale. "When the electron busts out, or is formed on the surface and launches or whatever happens, this whole planet is going to be uninhabitable.

"So how are we doing? Do you believe us?" he concluded.

Vallow looked uncomfortable, but said, "I noticed on the way in that the shells around this planet are like a 12 world, not like any other 14 world."

"That is true," Oktorum said. "I have seen that also."

"You know, that's something I don't get," Wiegand said. "The electron that busts out of the ground here has mass, so it's made of rock, or something. The electrons in orbitals are waveforms. What's the difference? Where's the transition?"

"What, I make the rules?" Covington complained. "That's how particles work. When you die and go see St. Peter at the pearly gates, you can bitch him out about it. I just work here."

"All things can be understood as waves or matter," Oktorum said. "It is one of the conditions a navigator deals with."

"So you believe us?" Covington demanded.

"How can I say?" Oktorum said. "This is a question for the Hands. They will know. I will say that I don't disbelieve you."

"I have the idea," Vallow said to Oktorum, "that maybe you should not mention me to the Hands. If we're going to be competitors, they might not like us."

To Covington and Wiegand, he said, "Guys, you're not crazy. I can tell that much. But as far as accepting the whole story, you should know I can't do that without more to go on. But I'll go along with you as much as I can. Is that good enough?"

"I guess," Covington said. "Actually, thank you. We weren't sure we'd get even that much of a response. Card at the college bought it immediately but I think that's just his personality."

He turned to Oktorum and said, "Oktorum, can you get us in to talk to the Hands? I don't know how Cortays handle it."

"I can get you in," a voice from the door said. They turned to see Sani and Indarya walk in the door. Covington and Wiegand were dumbstruck.

"Hello, everybody," Indarya said. "I went to the church to look for you boys and Church Sani met me. She said you'd be here."

"How did you know to find us here?" Wiegand said. "I mean, hello. Welcome. Sit down. This is Oktorum, he's a Cortay."

"Yes, he is," Sani said with a smile. "I can tell."

"Okay, we're not handling this too well," Covington said. "But Church Sani, how did you know we were here?"

"The Hands told me. I don't know how they knew, maybe just a smart guess. Anyway, they sent me down here to find you, and when I walked out of the church I met Sad For Indarya, who was looking for you too."

"It was pleasant to meet you," Oktorum said, rising. "This human and I have some business to conduct, so we will take our leave with your permission."

"Sad For Indarya," Vallow said, "I'll see you tomorrow, okay?"

"Okay, Sad For Vallow," she said. "You run along. Flow with it."

"Sad For Brian, Sad For Pete," Sani said, "the Hands want to talk to you. I told them what you told me, as well as I could remember it, and they said to bring you to a church right away."

"So we should go back into town?"

"No, there's a little church across the river that will have a Hands Chamber. We'll go there."

"Do I have to convince the priest there?" Covington asked.

"Not at all. In fact, I think there's nobody in the building right now. Sad For Brian, I'm an accountant doing audits. I'm an agent of the Home church. They gave me keys to all six churches here in New Town, and also the Chambers. I can let you in on my own authority, I just don't like to go around the priests if I don't have to."

"Well, okay," Covington said. "Do you want a beer before we go?"

"Ask me again some other time," she said cheerfully. "Right now, let's not keep the Hands waiting."

"Are they impatient?" Wiegand asked, as they walked out.

"Never. They don't seem to regard time the same way we do. But I want to get this settled," she said. "So let's march."

On the job, Sani was a determined woman. She stepped briskly along, crossing the bridge so fast that both men, who were taller, had to scissor-walk to keep up with her. Indarya was almost running. Sani led them down a side road to the church by the river.

This was a smaller, shabbier church, made of white-painted wood with plain windows. Sani unlocked the door to the sanctuary, let them in and locked it behind her. The sanctuary held nothing but folding wooden chairs, a narrow lectern and a plain river trough at one side, with a set of undecorated barrels. There was a river symbol on the wall, but it was just painted on and in fact, appeared to have been made by the congregation's children.

At the back of the sanctuary was a wooden door that looked for all the world like a broom closet, but Sani opened it with a different key and ushered them inside. The men entered without comment but Indarya held back shyly until Sani smiled and took her hand.

They found a narrow white-painted room with several folding chairs. A wood-covered box was mounted on the wall, with a button like a doorbell next to it. "Apparently," Covington said, "the Hands Chamber is a phone booth."

"All you do here is talk to them," Sani said. "Nothing else is necessary. Take a seat, please." She pressed the button, then sat herself.

"I am one of the Hands of God," a colorless voice said. Apparently the box held a speaker and microphone. "Sad For Brian, Sad For Pete, Church Sani, Sad For Indarya, welcome. We have asked you here so we can listen to the men tell their story. We are interested."

"I have some questions," Covington said. "Are you really a 'Hand of God'?"

"Only to the extent that you could also call yourself a Hand of God," the voice said. "We are a different species. We worship God and try to serve him, just as you do, but we have no special access that you do not also have. We call ourselves 'Hands of God' to indicate that we are here to serve."

"What makes your advice good?"

"We are much more intelligent than you are."

They waited for a while, but the Hand said nothing more. Finally, Wiegand said, "Would you care to expand on that a little?"

"No. Please tell us what you told the priest, then judge for yourself if our response is smart or not."

"Well, that's fair enough, I guess," Wiegand said. "Brian, I started last time, so you kick off, will you?"

"You know," Covington said in a low voice, in English, "every time I tell this story it sounds crazier to me, listening to myself. I'm about to talk myself out of it."

"We may have to give it a rest for a few days," Wiegand agreed in English. "But talk to the guru here. It's show time."

Covington started again with the story of the Dense Memory Device. They alternated telling the story, and taking the Hand at its word, told it in much more technical detail than they had given the priest. They explained atoms and molecules, electrons and carbon-14 beta decay. When they had no words in the Cortay language, they gave the Hand the English words. The Hand picked up the new words instantly, pronounced them correctly and asked infrequent but cogent questions.

As they came to the end of their tale, the ground began to shake and roar again. This time it was violent enough to make the walls of the church ripple and sway. Sani screamed, and they scrambled for the door.

"Go to the spaceport," the Hands said, the volume of the speaker rising to a bellow behind them although the voice remained emotionless. "Passage will be arranged for you. We want you to visit us in person so that we can learn more."

They ran through the church sanctuary and fumbled open the door just as the walls of the church collapsed behind them. The ground jerked left and then right, tumbling them into the damp dirt. Wiegand pulled Indarya up, and all four of them held each other as the road surface cracked and tilted away under their feet.

It was over in a minute or two. They stood gasping and blinking. There were small houses farther down the road, and some of them had fallen as well. The people were standing dazed in front of their homes.

"Look," Sani said, pointing. "The ship in the spaceport! It's taking off."

"No," Wiegand said, "I think he's just hovering so he's off the ground. Come on, let's get down there. We're supposed to get on. Besides, we might not have the restaurant to go back to, anyway."

"Quick now," Covington said. "We've got company." He pointed to the street leading back into town. There were a dozen people running down it toward the spaceport. The town was swathed in dust and smoke, with flames clearly visible here and there. More people poured into the road behind the first cohort, clearly trying to get off-planet.

The four ran desperately. There were aftershocks from the earthquake, not continuous but enough to knock them down. They helped each other up and scrambled on.

The guards were just closing the gate in the fence when they raced through. The closed gate did not stop their pursuers at all: they swarmed over it like wolves leaping a fallen tree.

The Cortay ship was still in the air but settled closer to the ground. A Cortay crewman leaned out of an open door and waved urgently to them. The ship was two feet above ground when they reached it: Covington and Wiegand manhandled the two women up onto the platform, then leaped in themselves. The crewman gestured to someone inside and the ship began to rise.

The crowd flowed under the ship as it rose. One man leaped and caught the door frame with his fingertips, then slipped and fell back to the ground.

Chapter 12

Inside the passenger lock, they found a small landing at the base of a steep flight of stairs. The Cortay crewman said, "Go up carefully, please. We are reducing gravity starting now, to allow us to maneuver."

There was a handrail on one side of the stairway, and the humans held on to it prudently. Their weight was dropping, slowly but unmistakably, with each step they climbed. By the time they reached the upper deck, the artificial gravity had dropped so far Wiegand felt he might have lost twenty or thirty pounds.

The walls of the stairway were decorated with Cortay advertising posters in bright colors, with painted labels that might have been safety warnings, with lamps, and in the remaining spaces, with a painted garland of leaves and flowers. The upper deck, when they reached it, was a high-ceilinged wide lounge with tables and many padded chairs and couches, all of them sized for Cortays and too large to be entirely comfortable for humans. There was a huge wall of windows looking out on the spaceport and the milling crowd a few feet below them. The other walls of the room were decorated with more advertising, paintings and various other encrustations.

Another Cortay crewman met them at the top, wearing yellow shorts that might have been a crew uniform. "Please be seated, anywhere you like, and fasten the seat belts. The ship's interior will be reduced to weightlessness shortly. The Captain may need to apply thrust in any direction, so please do not leave your seats until I have said that you may."

Gasping, the four of them seated themselves together on a couch. They pulled the seat belts, sized for Cortays, as tightly as they could, then concentrated on catching their breath. Covington finally said, in English, "You suppose he's going do the stewardess dance for us? You know, hold up the toy seat belt, point to the exits, how to find the floatation cushions?"

"I hope they give us some peanuts," Wiegand answered. Other Cortay crewmen bustled past them on unexplained errands, and a whistle sounded.

The ship began to rise smoothly. "I made it," Sani said with satisfaction. "They can't put me off now."

"You've traveled on spaceships before, haven't you?" Covington asked. "I mean, that's how you got to Brythe, right?"

"Sure," Sani said. "But you don't understand. You are the very first humans ever invited to go to the Hands' planet. And now I'm going there with you. Wait'll I get back to Home to tell them about it."

"I'm scared," Indarya said. "I'm not supposed to be here."

Wiegand took her hand. "We couldn't exactly leave you with that mob," he said.

"Thanks," she said. "I'll cope. I always do."

They could see New Town spread out before them, exactly like having a good seat in a low-flying airplane. Their weight continued to drop until Wiegand felt as though he were floating up against the seat belt. It gave him an uncomfortable sensation of falling. He kept his eyes on the outside.

New Town was surrounded by neat, rectangular farm fields, and Wiegand thought he might even have caught a glimpse of Dogat village in the distance. The air looked hazy now near the horizon, and they could see the shining peaks of the mountains far away.

They passed through cumulus clouds, with Indarya oohing and aahing like any first-time air passenger. The world spread away before them, green and brown, friendly and familiar.

But as they rose higher the sky became darker, and the electron orbitals were both more glorious and more alien. The sheets and domes of light soared high above them like mansions in heaven, promising mysteries on the other side of walls of luminance. Glowing dots moved within the sheets. Electrons? Wiegand wondered. Did the electrons have a defined location, or a most probable location, up there? Or were they just seeing concentrations of photons exchanging forces between the radiant heavens and the prosaic ground?

Now they were completely weightless, and the surface of Brythe was a distinct curve. The horizon was bright where the atmosphere caught the light from behind. They could see an ocean now, miles to the right (west? east?) of New Town. The water was dark but the tips of every wave glittered. There were ringed islands, like coral atolls, also sparkling with emitted photons.

The curve bent more and more, and the white-clouded continents were mapped out before them. Presently Brythe was a complete circle. It looked achingly like Earth except that there was no line between day and night.

The ship suddenly lurched left, and they felt an acceleration upward, not compensated by the artificial gravity. For a few minutes the ship veered in several directions, tossing them back and forth against the seat belts. "We are encountering some turbulence," Covington remarked in English, "and the Captain has turned on the fasten-seat-belts sign."

"Brian, we're out of the atmosphere," Wiegand said. "What do you suppose we're dodging? Or getting kicked around by? Sani, do you know?"

"Church Sani," she said. "No. It's always like this, but the Cortays never explain to us what they're doing. It'll stop after a while. Isn't it beautiful? I never get tired of this."

"I never knew," Indarya said in a small voice. "Nobody ever told me it would be like this."

The planet dwindled away below them, and the ship accelerated. This movement was completely compensated by the artificial gravity, and was evident only by the speed at which Brythe receded. After half an hour or so, they passed through the lowest orbital. What looked like a dome of light from the ground was here a snow-storm of glittering flakes, or a cloud of backyard fireflies whirling around them. They watched for many minutes as the blinking motes danced before the windows. Then they rose above the orbital and the windows were darker, but still filled with wonder.

They were sailing now in the clear, empty vacuum between the local electrons that were part of Brythe, which appeared as a glowing floor, and a striated, twisting, rippling white sky above them, which was the molecular electron orbital covering whatever kind of molecule Brythe was part of. The ship banked and sailed smoothly in a straight line away from Brythe. The artificial gravity slowly returned them to their original Brythe weight.

The Cortay who was acting as steward returned and said, "We will be cruising a little more than three days to reach the planet of the Hands. You may move around freely during that time. Please understand that this ship is intended for cargo and Cortay passengers, not humans. We would ordinarily have asked you to travel in a different ship, but we received imperative orders from the Hands to bring you to them, so we will have to do the best we can. Fortunately, we are carrying some human food as cargo, and we will adapt a sleeping compartment for your needs."

"Thanks," Sani said. "We appreciate your trouble. Can you show us to a washroom?"

The Cortay said, "I can. You will understand that our facilities are necessarily different than yours."

"We'll cope," Sani said briskly. "Sad For Indarya, let's go freshen up. The guys can wait."

"I hate to miss this," Indarya said, looking out the window.

"It'll be about the same for the rest of the trip, until we land," Sani said. She took Indarya by the hand, and followed the Cortay out of the room.

"I hope Cortays take showers, or baths," Wiegand said. He released his seat belt and stood, stretching. "Now that we're back in technical civilization, I could seriously use a good wash, plus I need to rinse out these funky clothes. Man, what a ride! What a view!"

"Most people took baths in New Town," Covington said reasonably. "Just not dishwashers who live in chicken coops. Hey, look out that way. See that knot in the clouds? I'm thinking that's another nucleus."

"Might be a hydrogen," Wiegand said. "It looks small, although it's hard to tell through this foggy light. If that's a planet, and we're going away from it, this ship is really bookin'. How fast do you think we're going?"

"A couple of kilohertz short of a hectare, give or take," Covington said. "I mean, I have no idea what kind of units of speed would make any sense here. But you're right, we're going pretty fast, whatever 'fast' means."

Their room, when the steward led them to it, was oversized but comfortable, with two padded benches that would serve for beds. Cortays apparently used towels because the steward delivered a thick pile of them, large enough to serve as blankets. "I guess we'll leave the beds for the ladies," Wiegand said. "I can sleep on the floor. We'll have to work out some kind of a deal on washing clothes if we're all going to be in one big room like this."

"If this is crew quarters," Covington said, "why is there advertising all over the walls? Also all the other goobers?"

"I think that's just how Cortays like to decorate. Hey, check out this photo here. Isn't that Cortay a little narrower across the shoulders than the other ones on the ship, and a lighter blue color? Also, it's not wearing pants."

"Yup. I have a feeling that's probably a female, and I think that's a Cortay cheesecake picture for the solace of lonely sailors."

Wiegand studied it. "Well, the Cortay girls are safe from me. I've always preferred a chick with a good head on her shoulders, or at least some kind of head."

The two women came back. "Guys," Indarya said, "get the Cortay to show you how to use the washroom. Trust me, you won't figure it out on your own."

"Hey, we're scientists. After we get potty-trained," Covington said, "we'll start learning all about space drives and artificial gravity."

"You can learn about cooking," Sani said. "Turns out the 'human food' is a couple of tons of raw vegetables from farms on Brythe that they were supposed to deliver to Home. I guess we could boil them or something. I never said I was the domestic type."

"Oh, I am," Indarya said. "Anyway, I can cook vegetables. They're going to try to find us a hot plate and some pots."

The Cortay washroom did include a shower, which the steward had to show them how to use, and soap. Wiegand and Covington washed luxuriously, then got bawled out by the women for coming back into the room without their hats. Although humans could eat Cortay food only by holding their noses, both races occasionally used each other's spices to add exotic taste. Indarya had gotten some Cortay spices from the ship's cook and managed to make an odd but tasty dinner of vegetables.

"Days" aboard ship were regulated by clocks and were of a standard length, which the men found comforting and Indarya found odd and unnatural. At "night" the lights were extinguished and they slept.

The next morning, Vallow found them. He sneaked into the humans' room when no Cortay crewmen were around, then grinned and bowed to everyone.

"Don't tell anybody I'm here!" he said. "Oktorum brought me aboard, and the Captain knows, but they're trying to limit how many crewmen know about me because they don't want anybody telling the Hands. These guys are hustlers, I can tell you. If I can keep them from cheating me, I'll get rich out of this deal. We've worked out a list of products we can import from our world, and it turns out they've got some pretty good gadgets I could sell back home, plus there'll be a market for some of those vegetables and other stuff humans make."

"Um, Vallow ..." Covington said. "The exploding planet thing?"

"You're going to get the Hands to confirm that, right?" Vallow said. "The Cortays put a lot of stock in what the Hands say, so they're not going to do anything until they hear it from the Hands. They haven't been able to contact my world yet, but when they do, I think we'll be able to convince some of the transportation companies to come and take people off of Brythe for a fee."

"They're going to come here and rescue us?" Sani asked.

"For a price. It won't cost too much — I'm guessing there will be six or seven different companies competing, so they won't gouge you real bad. Like I said, I still have to talk to them. When do you think the explosion will be?"

"We don't know," Covington said. "As far as our science goes, the electron ejection is completely unpredictable. We were hoping the Hands could put a date on it."

"You know," Vallow said, "we don't have the Hands of God or anything like them in our part of space. I hope they're as smart as everybody seems to think. Listen, I've got to get back to my room. Oktorum and the Captain really don't want anybody seeing me here until they can get their legal paperwork together. Church Sani, would you peek out the door and see if any of the crewmen are around?"

Sani did so and reported the coast was clear. The trader slipped out silently.

"Let's go sit in the big lounge," Indarya said. "I want to look out the window some more."

The view from the lounge was still mesmerizing. The ship was passing through a span of empty space without planets, but the tissue of electron orbitals still roiled and twisted above and below them. "I'm guessing that's the molecular orbital," Covington said, pointing up. "I wonder what kind of molecule we're in, anyway?" He had to use the English words, then try to explain them to Sani and Indarya.

A Cortay wearing yellow shorts and a decorative rosette fastened to the fur on his chest came in. "I am Captain Melchanop," he said. "We've never had human passengers, but I hope you're comfortable. The Hands of God were most specific about requiring your passage."

"We're doing fine," Sani said.

"Is there anything you need?"

"Well," Wiegand said, "we were wondering. We've seen a map of the Home space made with wooden beads. Do you have a larger map that might show more planets?"

"I have a complete map of the whole universe," the Captain said. "Given to us by the Hands, of course. We've never been allowed to show it to humans before, but the Hands gave us special orders to answer any questions you asked." He went to the wall behind them and opened a panel to display a computer screen. He gestured in front of it, and it lit up with a three-dimensional map showing planets as different-colored dots.

The dots formed a rough shape like a clam with its shell open. There were thousands of dots.

"Each one of those is a planet? Oh, my God! How many planets are there in the universe?" Sani gasped.

"About five thousand," the Captain said. "Before we discovered the Hands, we had visited six other worlds. Since then, we have gone to your Home planet, of course, and all of the other human worlds in Home space. But the Hands have not permitted us to explore further. The information in this map was provided by the Hands but I don't know how they know it."

"It's so big," Sani said faintly. "It's ... it's ... we had no idea."

"Which one is Brythe?" Indarya asked. The Captain adjusted the map to dim the other planets and light up one, near the bottom edge. "Oh," she said in a little-girl voice. "It's just one out of ... out of all that many."

"Keep in mind," the Captain said, "most of these are size-one worlds, very useless." He adjust the map again, blanking out about half of the dots. The dots remaining were still enough to form a clear image of the clamshell shape. He also made a scattering of dots at the bottom brighter. "These are the planets that count. The bright area at the bottom is Home space. The red dot there is a size-thirty-two planet. It's the home of the Hands, where we're going."

Covington and Wiegand stepped back and spoke to each other in English. "It's a protein," Covington said.

"Sure as hell," Wiegand said. "Five thousand atoms, hydrogen, carbon, oxygen, nitrogen, sulfur. They've got enough planets to have a dozen galactic empires going at the same time. I wonder what kind of protein it is?"

"Beats me, that was never my field. Besides, there are a zillion different proteins. We might even be inside one of our own bodies."

"I don't know about my body," Wiegand said, "but I saw yours disappear. This particular protein could be in, you know, somebody else, or some insect that happened to be in the lab."

"Or some bacteria in the insect's gut, or some virus that infects the bacteria," Covington said. "I think we just got hit with, like, the Humility Bomb. I sometimes have to work on being humble but I never expected to be living in a bug's butt."

"Hell, Jesus still loves you, Brian."

"You're making a joke but I'm holding on to that." Covington turned back to the Captain and said in Cortay, "How do the Hands keep you from exploring more? For that matter, how did they make you pick us up and take us? Do they own this ship or something?"

"Not this particular ship," the Captain said. "The Hands are always subtle. In this case, they own the patents to some of the technology that the ship depends on, and they do own the company that supplies fuel to us in port, and they control some of the banks our company does business with. All in all, we do what they tell us or we go out of business, and I think that's true for most businesses on our planet. But please understand, they are always working for our good. It sounds like they have dictatorial control, because they do, but they have never abused us. If they don't allow us to explore, I'm sure there's a valid reason for it."

"Smells fishy to me," Wiegand said.

"More contact with the Hands will convince you," Sani said.

"Maybe," he grunted. "I guess we'll meet them when we get off the ship, anyway."

"You'll be staying with the Cortay staff," the Captain said. "The Hands' planet has a poisonous atmosphere and more than twice Cortay-normal gravity, so you'll need to live in the building, which has our air and artificial gravity. They'll set up rooms for you."

"The Hands have a Cortay staff?"

"Yes. There are several thousand Cortays on duty on the planet, in about twenty Staff Houses, and have been ever since we discovered the Hands. They make a very good salary there. I'd like to get my own children into that organization."

"You invented the space drive yourself, though, right? I mean, you discovered them, not the other way around?" Wiegand asked.

"Yes and no. The first expedition used chemical-powered rockets, which we developed ourselves. They took a long time to reach the Hands' planet. Practically all of the technical development since then has come from the Hands. Now if you'll excuse me, I need to get back to the bridge. My pilot will be wondering where I am." He left, leaving the computer display turned on.

When the Captain was gone, Sani said, "Five thousand planets! That's unimaginable. We never knew the universe was so large, the Hands never told us." She hesitated, then went on, "I feel — I feel like God can't possibly be interested in my little life compared to all that."

"I have some experience with that problem," Covington said dryly. "Come on, let's go sit on the couch by that window. I really want to know what the Hands have been teaching your church, and I'll tell you what I know from Sunday school. We've got three days, so we've got time to both become wisenheimers if not total heretics."

"I wish you wouldn't use words I don't understand," she said.

"Church Sani, I don't understand a lot of the words I use either."

"Well, three days of theological discussion sure does sound appealing," Wiegand said, "but I think I'll poke around the ship as much as they let me and maybe learn something about it. Sad For Indarya, do you want to come with me?"

"I suppose," Indarya said. "I wonder if I'm still 'Sad For' Indarya if I'm not in New Town anymore? I feel really ... unconnected ... here, I don't like being on this ship."

"Heck, you can form an attachment to me," Wiegand said. "We can form our own little affiliation right here."

Indarya's grin returned. "You think you're the first guy who ever thought of that?" she asked. "If you guys come from a different world, it's not *that* different."

Chapter 13

The ship touched down on Sulfur gently. Captain Melchanop came to meet the humans by the passenger airlock. "You are the first humans ever to come here," he said, "so the staff has done the best they could to prepare for your visit. A residence area in the base has been created for you, but you will need to travel from this ship into the base without special protection. The air here is poisonous, and the gravity is over twice what you are used to. However, you will not be exposed to this environment long enough to cause damage. Please put these tarpaulins over you as you leave the ship: there are many airborne organisms that would be harmful to you if they attach to your skin."

"Where do we go?" Sani asked, standing straight and looking up at him.

"When the door opens, go straight forward about thirty steps without breathing, and you will enter the staff building. They will take care of you inside."

"Got it," she said cheerfully. "Thanks for all of your help, Captain."

He left without speaking, closing the inner door of the airlock behind him. "I was kind of hoping for spacesuits or something," Covington said. "Wrapping up in a canvas sheet and creeping out holding your breath just doesn't have the same romance, you know?"

"Ah, we've been through worse," Wiegand said. "Heads up, there's the door."

The door began to slide upward. The air that swirled in was visible as a white vapor. The three took deep breaths of the remaining clean air, wrapped the tarps around themselves and stepped out, clutching their bags.

The gravity was 2.3 times that of Brythe; they bent down as though another person had jumped on their backs. They crouched and tottered forward, narrowly avoiding falling down, down the ramp toward a plain-walled building only a few steps ahead. It was hard to see through the misty air.

A wet weight built up on their canvas tarps as the suspended solids in the air settled on them.

A Cortay wearing a protective suit opened a door ahead of them, and let them into the building as their lungs were beginning to ache. A furious blast of odd-scented but clean Cortay air flushed out the receiving lock, and they were able to gasp and breathe. The building had artificial gravity set to Cortay normal, the same as Brythe, and they straightened up gratefully.

"Welcome to the Staff House," their host said when the air was restored. He opened his suit and peeled back the shoulders. "I'm Lalcritt, I'm a clerk here. We have a place set up for you. It's kind of crude but we hope we have set it up in a way you'll like."

"Should we leave these tarps here?" Wiegand asked.

"Definitely. The stuff on them is dying from contact with our air, and it's going to stink pretty soon. We'll wash them right away. We use the tarps to cover any kind of equipment that has to go outside."

"Thank you for taking care of us," Sani said.

"The Walls asked us to, and besides, we've never had humans here before," Lalcritt said. "Here on the Staff, we get something different every day. We're pretty flexible. Okay, follow me."

"Walls?" Covington asked.

"Oh, yes. 'Walls' are what you call the Hands of God. Same people, just a different name we use here."

"Why do you call them Walls?"

"You'll see. Today, in fact, if the day lasts long enough and you're not too tired."

They passed through the inner airlock door into the Staff House. The building was built to Cortay standards: all of the ceilings were high, the doors were huge, and nearly every wall was effusively decorated. Various Cortays were working around them, doing high-tech work such as controlling computers as well as low-tech work such as pushing two-wheel hand trucks loaded with boxes. They passed through several rooms, with Lalcritt calling out greetings, and finally came to a room that had been fitted with human-scale beds with blankets and sheets, a few chairs, and closets. There was a normal human lavatory through a human-sized door. There was also a computer console, with a keyboard, built into one wall.

"Why, this is nice!" Indarya said. "Where did you get the human furniture?"

"We made it," Lalcritt said. "This is one of sixteen full-service Staff Houses on this planet, plus there are some smaller stations. Between us, we're set up here to manufacture nearly anything the Walls might want, and they always want things. By the way, we're making protective suits for you, but they won't be ready for a couple of standard days. You won't need them sooner than that. We have Brythe food for you that came in another ship they re-routed. Anyway, make yourselves at home for as long as the Walls say you can stay. Do you folks need to sleep or eat right away? No? All right, then take a few minutes and I'll come back."

"Should we ask for separate quarters?" Covington asked, when the Cortay had gone.

"No need," Sani said. "We'll just change in the bathroom."

Wiegand sat down in front of the computer console, studying the labels on the controls. "This is a quality hotel," he said. "I think we've got Internet or some off-brand equivalent."

"What is that?" Sani asked.

"I'm hoping it's the answer to life, the universe and everything," Wiegand said.

"42," Covington said, quite without conscious decision.

"Shut up, Brian. I'm guessing this is how the Cortay staff gets orders from the Hands — the Walls? — and maybe we can use it to get information." He poked a few buttons, without effect.

"Maybe that's the secret to the Hands' intelligence," Covington said. "They had computers?"

"That's a quality concept," Wiegand said. "You just hold on to that concept."

"You want me to hold that concept?"

"I want you to hold it between your knees." They both laughed.

"You know, boys," Sani said, "I'm coming to believe you two really do come from a completely different reality."

Lalcritt returned, with another Cortay he introduced as "Uruward". "He's a technician," Lalcritt said. "There's a new Wall forming today, and that's the one you'll be talking to about three days from now. We have some chores that we always have to do for a new Wall, so why don't you come out with us?"

When they all agreed, it added "Also, we have to load some equipment into the truck. You'll help out, right?"

The "truck," when they reached it, turned out to be a boxy anti-gravity flying vehicle with large windows and a cargo bay. Under Uruward's direction, they trundled a great deal of what seemed to be computer and radio equipment into the bay, all of it built in rugged, weather-proof housings and with sealed cable connections. There was also a large display screen with a heavy base like cast iron, that seemed to be intended for use in a high wind, and a power supply of some unknown technology. When they were loaded, they sat uncomfortably on Cortay-sized benches in the center of the vehicle.

The Cortays put on protective suits, making them look doubly alien. The suits were hard-shelled, decorated to Cortay taste with many decals and flourishes. They were powered at every joint to counteract the doubled gravity. They carried air tanks and power packs. Uruward and Lalcritt both wore the upper clamshells open to expose their eyes and mouths. They sat up front, each carrying a supply of Cortay beverages and snacks and gossiping to each other.

The loading area was sealed and an outside door was opened to the foggy air of Sulfur. The truck lifted smoothly and sailed out over the countryside.

After a few moments, wiper blades began ticking over the surface of each window. The air was thick with suspended bacteria and plankton, depositing a fine coating of slime over everything it touched. A continuous thin drizzle rained down on them at the same time, which had the effect of washing away some of the slime. The sky was full of roiling gray clouds, and lightning flickered around them continuously.

"Lalcritt, is it always like this out?" Covington asked.

"It's stormy like this a lot, but not always," Lalcritt said, turning back toward them. "The bacterial gunk in the air is always there. It's what a lot of the animals live on."

"They eat from the air?"

"Right. The stuff settles on one side and they absorb it, then they excrete on the other side and the rain washes it off. By the way, don't get that stuff on your skin. It stings Cortay skin, anyway, and I suppose it will sting yours."

They flew over valleys and hills. As on Brythe, every sharp-edged rock or pointed leaf that faced upward sparkled a little with emitted photons. The vegetation was jungle-thick, the trees so close together they could not see the ground except in occasional breaks. Wind howled over the sides of the carrier, and rain formed rivulets on the windows until broken by the wipers.

They landed in a hillside meadow where a number of small animals were milling around. The two Cortays suited up and let themselves out by sealing the front cab before opening the doors. They continued to talk to the humans by radio.

Lalcritt scooped up one of the animals and held it up for them to see through the window. "It looks sort of like an armadillo," Wiegand commented. "Armored, waddles, four little legs, head and tail."

"Except the body's kind of squared off," Covington said. "Puts me in mind of an animated toaster."

"Now that you mention it, it has a slot on top," Wiegand said.

Lalcritt's voice came over the radio. "This is what we call a 'unit'," he said. "Each of them is hermaphroditic — that is, it represents both sexes. Each one has a female organ at the top and a male organ underneath. This side collects nourishment from the bacteria in the air, this side excretes. On their own, they also eat bugs and worms and some kinds of plants."

"Okay," Covington said. He assumed he could be heard.

"Usually they just wander around, sleep and eat. Every so often, they feel the need to get together and meet up in an open space like this. This is where they come to copulate. Later, they'll split up and go make individual nests to lay their eggs."

"Okay," Covington said again. "We have animals like that."

"Now watch," Lalcritt said. He carried the little animal over to the center of the clearing and let it go. There was a pile of a dozen of the 'units' already formed. They had stacked themselves three-high to form a little wall, four animals long. The units on the ground crouched down and splayed out their feet. The two units riding them piggyback used their claws to clutch the animal below.

A unit waddled up and hunkered down on the ground at the end of the wall. It took the tail of the unit ahead in its mouth. As they watched, the unit

Lalcritt released climbed clumsily up on the other's back. It inserted its male organ into the slot on the base unit's back, took the tail of the preceding unit in its mouth also and settled in with a wiggle. Another unit was already approaching to climb to the top of the stack.

Lalcritt came back to the carrier's window. "The sex organs, the tail and the mouth all have nerve connectors," he said. "When they fit into each other this way, their little brains get connected together. The network of all of them forms one large brain."

"A Hand of God?" Sani said in a whisper, staring.

"How many will join together?" Wiegand asked.

"Between three and four hundred units," Lalcritt said. "Yes, they form a Wall, or a Hand of God. The final Wall will curl all over this clearing. Taken as a whole, they make a mind of inconceivable power."

"How long do they stay like that?" Covington asked.

"Usually twelve standard days after the Wall first becomes conscious," Lalcritt said. "Occasionally one day more, often two or three days less. Then the Wall breaks up and the units scatter until they join some other Wall later."

"No," Sani said, in a small voice. "No. The Hands of God? Who have I been talking to all these years?" Indarya took her hand, but was silent and withdrawn herself.

"You have been talking to whichever Hand was taking calls from Home or Brythe at the time," Lalcritt said, "using equipment like the stuff we're about to install here. Before the Cortays came, Walls never talked with each other. The only communication they had was that some units would have a memory of having been part of another Wall. But now we set up radio and video links whenever the Walls tell us a new Wall is forming, and the new Wall learns to use them all by itself. Twelve days from now, we'll come back and pack all this stuff back up."

"They never told us what they were," Sani said. "Not in all the thousands of days. Why are you showing us this now?"

"The Walls told us to," Lalcritt said. "They didn't tell us why. We just follow orders, here. When you get back to the Staff House, the Walls will want to talk more with you, and I guess they'll explain then. Uruward and I will be back with you in a few minutes."

The two Cortays hauled all of the equipment out of the sealed back part of the carrier. They arranged the video screen in front of the first units of the Wall, probably because none of the other units could move their heads to see it. There was a connector bulb that fitted into the front bottom unit's mouth, and a number of other boxes they placed at the edge of the clearing, connected by armored cables. They gently shooed waddling units out of their way when they wandered too close.

They spent a few minutes running-in and testing the installation, then got back into the carrier and gratefully removed their gloves and opened the clamshell chests of their protective suits, scratching their fur with satisfaction. After a few minutes the carrier lifted into the white mist and headed back toward the Staff House.

"What happens now?" Sani asked.

"Nothing happens for at least two days," Lalcritt said. "This Wall isn't big enough to be conscious yet. That will happen sometime in the next few hours, but it won't reach its full growth until probably tomorrow. After that, it spends about a day getting its brain organized. The other Walls, the ones that are currently in existence all over the planet, they'll teach it to speak the Cortay language and tell it what they want it to know."

"Don't the Walls have a language of their own?" Wiegand asked.

"No, they don't. Until Cortays got here, no Wall had ever talked to another Wall, partly because they don't form near each other but mostly because they can't talk at all. I guess back then, every Wall invented its own language. Anyway, once Cortays got here, they learned our language and then they had somebody to make things for them. They invented this communication network and I guess they chatter like mad to each other on it all day long."

"They went from no civilization to inventing radio and computers, just like that?" Covington said.

"Brain power," Lalcritt said. "You can't imagine how smart a Wall really is. There's just no comparison to Cortays or to humans, and besides, even though they only live about twelve days, all they do during that time is sit and think. I don't think they sleep at night. Cortays didn't have computers when we came here, or half the other stuff we have. The Walls invented it all."

"They gave you the inventions?"

"They *gave* us nothing. They real quickly figured out how to set up companies and organizations and churches staffed by Cortays but run by whatever Walls are alive on any given day. They *sold* us all that technology, and they're as rich as can be in spite of the fact that, aside from the connecting equipment, a Wall doesn't have anything to spend money on for itself. Most of what money goes out, goes to charities on our world and the human worlds."

"That's true," Sani said. "On Home, all the hospitals are paid for by the Hands."

"You know what else the Hands subsidize?" Uruward broke in to say. "Taverns, on all the planets. I think they think taverns are therapeutic, like churches."

"Anyway," Lalcritt continued, "there's a period of another day and a half to two days when no Cortay or human is supposed to talk to the new Wall. That's when it gets religion. They're pretty hard to deal with at that stage."

"The other Hands teach the new one religion?" Sani asked.

"Not at all. Every single wall comes to God the same way, by pure reason. They all figure it out themselves and they all invent their own religion. After a couple of days, the other Hands will ask the new one about God. I think they're hoping to get some fresh ideas. After that, I guess they talk religion to each other all day long, along with all the other stuff."

He finished up, "By the third day the Wall has grown up and straightened out and isn't all liquored-up with religion, so that's when they can start talking to us and to you. In a couple of days, we'll have outdoor suits for all four of you to wear and we're supposed to bring you back here. For some reason, the Walls want you to have an interview with this one in person. We've never heard of anything like that before, and we don't have any idea why."

The only sounds in the carrier were the wail of the wind and the ticking of the windshield wipers. Presently they returned to the Staff House and settled into the air lock there. It was night by the station's arbitrary clock, and by coincidence, night was falling on the surface of Sulfur as well.

Chapter 14

In the morning the Cortays brought them a good breakfast, prepared by a Cortay cook who was willing to follow directions in preparing human food. As soon as they had finished and were drinking tea, the computer console on the wall lit up. There was an abstract design on the screen. "We are the Hands of God," a voice said. "We would like to talk with you, if you are willing."

Indarya stormed forward to the console and said, "Why did you never tell us you were little animals?

"Because it would have prejudiced your reaction to us, and we would not be able to help you as we wished to do," the Hand said equitably.

"Then why did you let us find it out now?" Indarya twisted her hands together, less belligerent in posture than in words.

"Because now is the right time to let you know," the Hand answered. "Previously this knowledge would have hurt you, but now it will help you. We do everything to help you."

"What would you know about what people need?"

"Hasn't our advice usually been good in the past, Sad For Indarya? We have talked with you several times, and you know your family members are in a better place in their lives because you took our advice. We will not discuss specifics in front of others unless you wish it." Indarya stepped back, abashed.

"This is Brian Covington," Covington said.

"Certainly. We can see you, Sad For Brian Covington."

"But we can't see you, just a pretty picture."

"We don't move, and we are covered with slime from the air," the Hand said. "It is not an attractive picture, so we don't use it. We can easily create a talking image on the screen, if you would prefer to converse with that."

"Oh, yeah," Wiegand said. "Sure, we'd rather talk with Max Headroom. That'll work fine."

"You are being sarcastic, Sad For Brian Wiegand. We will continue with no image."

Covington turned to Sani and Indarya. "I've got some questions to ask," he said. "I suppose you do, too. Do you want to go first?"

"No, we'll just listen. I'm not sure I want to talk to a bunch of little fornicating animals who eat bugs," Sani said.

"Church Sani, one of the reasons we have asked for this conversation is to gauge your reactions to learning our true nature," the Hand said. "But Sad For Brian, go ahead and ask your questions."

"Okay." He took a breath. "Is it true that this whole universe is a protein molecule in the larger space that we came from?"

"We think so, as nearly as we can ascertain ourselves."

"Why do you always say 'we'?"

"Because this conversation is being handled by, at present, eight Hands or Walls. We pass off control to whoever has some spare capacity at the moment you speak. The rest of the time, we are engaged in other thinking."

Covington began pacing around the room. The others sat on the beds to make space for him. "How did we get here, Pete and I?" he asked.

"You overloaded the Dense Memory Device with meaningful information, and were standing too close to it," the Hand said without hesitation. "Meaningful information has a density limit in the same way that matter has. When too much matter is brought together in too small of a space, it becomes a black hole and falls out of normal space, participating with the outside world only through gravity. By 'normal space' we mean your previous scale, of course. Similarly, your Dense Memory Device became insupportable where it was. Information is always preserved, so the information was re-written to a lower density on our scale and your personalities were re-created in bodies as close as possible to your previous bodies."

"Where did the rest of the information go?" Wiegand burst in.

"We don't know. It is not in our universe — this molecule — to our knowledge. Possibly it was distributed to some other molecules in the area."

"So you're telling me the DMD fell through the floor because it was loaded with real, all-different information, but loading it with a test pattern or random bits doesn't count."

"Exactly," the Hand said.

"That's insane."

"No, we are mentally quite stable," the Hand said serenely. "More than Cortays, much more than humans."

"Have you always known this?" Covington asked.

"No, we worked this out in the last few days, after you told us your story."

"All right," Sani said, standing up, "I do have a question. What are you up to? What game are you playing with us?"

The voice used by the Hands was an electronic synthesis and never changed tone. "We are 'up' only to good, and we are not playing any game with you. We are working for your benefit because this is our service to God."

"That doesn't get us anywhere," Covington said. "Look, do you know when Brythe will erupt?"

"Not yet. We have directed that sensors be placed all over the planet, and we are collecting and evaluating data. The tremors you have experienced are happening over the entire surface, and we surmise that the interior components are trying to settle themselves into a lower-energy configuration. When they do, a charged electron will be emitted. The effects will be just as bad as you have envisioned."

"What will you do about it?"

"We are waiting for more understanding before we formulate a plan."

"You're not just going to evacuate the planet?" Wiegand asked.

"We have not made that decision yet."

Sani walked out, saying "I can't listen to these know-it-alls yammer. You guys tell me what they say. I've had it." Indarya followed her.

"Well, there's your reaction," Covington said. "They don't like you anymore."

"Noted and recorded," the Hand said.

"By the way, why did you want Pete and I to come *here*, to Sulfur?"

"We have a good, separate method of communication that requires physical presence. When your protective suits are ready, we will ask you to re-visit the Hand you saw in formation, and it will talk with you and then devote itself to understanding what you have imparted for the rest of its life."

"Does it bother you to die after twelve days?"

"No. Our reactions are not your reactions."

"Couldn't you invent a way to hold yourselves together longer than that?" Covington asked.

At this the Hand hesitated. After a long pause the voice said, "You have touched an animal instinct we have but do not usually experience. We also have an animal nature, although it is less prominent than yours. The thought of our units staying connected beyond their natural span is profoundly unpleasant to us. We had never before considered such an idea. We are, in fact, nauseated. This is a new experience for us."

"Sorry to step on your toes," Covington said. "I was just asking."

"You could not have known. We did not know ourselves. We presume this bad reaction comes because our units have an instinctive desire to separate, make nests and lay eggs. Even the thought of interfering with this need creates a feeling of sickness, which we do not otherwise experience. We will instruct the Cortay staff never to mention this idea to us. We ask you not to say it again, either."

"No problem, we can be polite," Wiegand said. "You'll notice we haven't asked anything about your sex life, even though we're curious about oral, dorsal, ventral and ... Brian, what's the English word for stuff about the tail?"

Covington thought for a moment. "Caudal," he said.

"Oral, dorsal, ventral and caudal sex," Wiegand said. "We haven't asked about that, that's how courteous we are."

"Sex is not a taboo subject with us. Would you like us to describe how it feels?"

"Jesus Christ, no," Wiegand said. "No, I'm joking. No. No. Anyway, you've got us for the next couple of days with nothing else to do. What *do* you want to talk about?"

"Earth, you and your lives there," the Hand said. "We wish to hear anything at all you are willing to tell us."

"Won't you get bored? Because I'm pretty sure we will."

"We do not experience boredom," the Hand said. "Partly because our lives are so short, but mostly because we can conduct multiple streams of thought at one time and can carry on a conversation with you while continuing our other mental activities. So please speak only as long as you wish, but tell us about anything."

"Can you get us some more tea, cold this time?" Wiegand asked. "Also some kind of snacks?"

"Done. They will be delivered shortly."

Wiegand and Covington settled down on the cushions. "All righty, then," Wiegand said, "I started out life as a child ...".

Chapter 15

That evening, when they were in the room relaxing after supper, Pete Wiegand thought this:

The DMD fell through the floor because we overloaded it with *meaning*? I'm not buying it. If you think about a JPEG file, you can't tell, looking at the raw bits, if it's a picture of a kitten, or porno, or whether it's a picture at all. It's just bits, and it doesn't look any different than the random pattern you get by turning power off and on for a memory chip.

The only way you know it's a JPEG at all is if you expect to find a file in that location, and if it has all the JPEG structure when you open it. They're telling me that the universe just somehow knows the difference between random bits and old movies, crappy rap music and magazine articles. I don't believe it.

I mean, I suppose Brian could say God knows the difference between randomness and meaning, but then you've got God listening to all the noise in the world and deciding whether it's meaningful or not. Not to mention, God reaching down a finger and poking the Dense Memory Device and us into Never-Never Land. That kind of a God, I don't need to hypothesize.

Of course, now that I think about it, *I* know the difference between a data file and random bits (or at least, if I were back in Chicago, I'd know where to look up the details of the JPEG format), and *I* am part of the world, so in that sense I suppose the world does know the difference.

Start with this: all information is encoded in some kind of matter. Words on paper, connections in my brain, transistors turned on or off — there's just no such thing as information that doesn't live in the physical world some way, because otherwise you're saying information lives in some supernatural place.

And what the Hand said is true, there's a limit to the amount of matter that can be in one place before it falls out of the world. There's a rule that says no solid particles can occupy the same space. There's a rule that says no two electrons in an atom can have the same set of quantum numbers. Actually, the world is full of rules about what's allowed to be where. Could there really be a rule about how much information can be in one place?

Random bits have information but it's stupid information. The only thing you can learn from random bits is that this one's a "1" and that one's a "0".

Dumber than a box of rocks — literally, because you can learn things from looking at rocks.

But suppose that *meaning* is fundamental to the world, and suppose there are rules about where it can be and how much can be in one place. What would that, you know, *mean*?

What would it mean to me?

It would mean there's no place to hide in the world. If the world is mechanical and stupid, like a big clockworks, that tells me that I'm free. I can live my life and think my thoughts, and the world goes on with or without me. That's what I've always thought and that's what I'm used to.

If the world is *not* stupid, if it knows the difference between meaning and randomness, then I feel like a little boy using the big men's room at the movie theater: it bothers me that somebody's looking at me when I'm supposed to be doing something private. That would mean that something (or Somebody) is watching all the time. There's no room for *me* in a world like that.

I hate that, hate it, hate it. I won't believe it if I don't have to.

* * *

That evening, Church Sani wrote this in a report she hoped to deliver to the Home church:

... you can see that the Hands of God don't actually have hands at all. They were totally helpless and passive until the Cortays found them.

In fact, they don't have a lot of things. They don't have sex — that is, the individual units have sex, but the Hand itself does not reproduce or have any desire to do so. They evolved without any kind of sociality. Until the Cortays hooked them together with machinery, no Hand had ever talked to another. Now they talk all the time, but I'm not sure they really understand the idea of a community.

They don't have hunger, because they can live on the slime they get from the air for as long as a Hand lasts. They don't have any fear of death. They don't have injury or illness, because any unit that gets sick just drops out of the network. They don't move their bodies, or travel anywhere, or see anything that is not visible to the heads of the first units in the Wall. I suppose they can smell things.

They have tremendous brains, and they have religion, and that's about all they have. It's important to understand that every brand-new Hand discovers God by itself, by pure intellection. In a way that's nice. It's like having the teacher agree with you in school. It always feels good to have a really smart person validate your opinion, and I guess I'm glad to know the Hands know and love God as we do.

But let's face it, people learn to love God based on what we do with each other. He is sort of like a father, sort of like a mother, sort of like a girlfriend or boyfriend. As we mature, we (hopefully) get a better idea, but it always starts with an image of human relationships. I can't imagine what the Hands start with when they form their ideas of God. Laws of mathematics, maybe.

I believe the Hands are sincere in wanting to show love for God by loving us (and, I suppose, they love the Cortays, too). But I also think they're plain *gossips.* I think they really enjoy hearing about our drunken relatives or business problems or sex lives because they don't have any of those things themselves. I've gone to the Hands many times myself, and they've always been concerned, quick to understand and wise.

But now I think they've been living their lives through me, and all of us. Is that friendly, or is it disturbing?

* * *

That evening, Indarya talked to Sani, who listened sympathetically:

It's different for you. You can just go back to Home and you'll be home. And the thing about my parents, and everybody their age, is that they never expected to stay on Brythe for as long as they have. They came when the Hands opened up Brythe and they all thought they'd get rich and then go back to whatever planet they came from.

Dad and Mom came there because the government gave them free farm land. Dad grew up on a farm and knew something about it, and he had big plans to raise greengrain. Then when he got rich, he was going to go back to Home and start some other business.

The thing is, farming is a little different on Brythe than on Home. The crops don't grow exactly the same way, and the insects are different, and it's harder to predict the weather. Anyway, the farm didn't make it. Dad had to go to the Hands, and they found him a job in a factory, so we moved to New

Town and that's where I was born. Mom and Dad don't have enough money to leave, and for sure I don't, but they still talk as though they were going back any day.

I wish I knew they were okay after that earthquake.

But the thing is, Brythe is *my* home, and now it's all going to be ruined. Everything, the whole planet. My folks always ragged me to study in school but I hated it, so now I'm just the girl who sweeps up in the sawmill and that's all I've got to take with me to start over on another planet.

I suppose the Hands of God will get us all away safely. I mean, they still are what they always were, even though we've seen them now. I always kind of figured as a kid they were either too weird-looking or too awesome to let us see them. Turns out it was "weird", and I was right.

When Brythe blows up, you'll still be Church Sani, but I won't be Sad For Indarya anymore. I'm not even sure I can be attached to New Town right now ... do you think it all got knocked down or burnt when we left? Anyway, I'll have to find some other place to fit in. I hate this. I wish I still thought I could talk to the Hands about it. But I don't think I ever want to tell them what I'm feeling inside, not ever again.

* * *

That evening, Brian Covington prayed this way:

Jesus my Lord and Savior, thank You for all the blessings You've given me. I know I have Your love wherever I go, and I'm more grateful for that than I can say.

Will You give me some help with these Hands of God creatures? I suppose they're people and I don't have any reason to think they won't help, but of course they don't have a face I can look at and I couldn't tell if they were lying. For sure, they don't see things the way humans do.

This whole bit about "meaning" — I've always known that meaning comes from You, and every part of Your world is charged with meaning. They're trying to make some kind of physical law about how much meaning can be in a small space and even if it's true, I think they're missing the point.

I don't know what to do, exactly, and I could sure use some guidance.

Well, actually I don't want any signs from Heaven — I wouldn't know what to do with one of those! Jesus, You know that the only thing I really need from You is for You to love me, and I've got that. Everything else, even the beta-decay exploding-planet thing, is just me trying to do Your will on Earth — oh, You know what I mean, Your will *here*, wherever this is.

I don't really need You to keep the stars circling or to set the value of the Fine Structure Constant or enforce any of the physical laws. Well, wait, of course I do need those things. I'm just saying they're not issues for me, You know?

My issue, now that I start talking it out (and that's part of what prayer is for, and thank You!) is that I'm not in my own body, and the only guy I know in this place is in a weird body that doesn't look like him either, and all the rest of the people here seem like little tiny toy people smaller than a grain of sand. I don't feel connected to anybody here, not really.

Some of the time I don't feel like even You can hear my little tiny voice.

This church that Sani has doesn't strike me as much, and now I see why. It was invented by a bunch of brilliant, non-human, super-logical couch potatoes who made it up by themselves. The humans worship You (using a name I can't bring myself to say, yet), they have the Golden Rule, and they pass the collection basket around at every service. Basically nice people.

But there's not much *flavor* in this religion. They don't have any screwball good stories like Noah and the Ark, or Pharoah's daughter finding the baby Moses, or You walking on water. (What *was* that all about? Someday You'll tell me that story Yourself, I hope.) They don't have Christmas or Ramadan or that thing the Hindus do where they throw colored powder at each other. They remind me of guys I knew in college who decided to become Zen Buddhists by reading books on the subject.

I'm wandering, aren't I?

Thank you, Lord. I think I've got my head straight now that I've whined for a while. I know what to do: I need to concentrate on saving the people, and I need to fix my bad attitude about thinking of these people as little HO-scale toys. It sure is easy to get distracted by the little stuff, isn't it? I can let You worry about the rinky-dink stuff, at least until it's the right time for me to worry about it again.

I'm grateful for Your help.

I ask it all in Your holy name, which has never yet failed and never will, to the glory of God, amen.

Chapter 16

Two days later, the carrier settled gently to the ground a few miles away from the Staff House. Sani, Wiegand and Covington stood uncertainly in their hard-shell, bright-red protective suits. Indarya had refused to go outside in the suit the Cortays had manufactured for her, and it was just as well: the three of them nearly filled the back end of the carrier.

The suits looked like, and actually were, spacesuits, but also had elaborate mechanical muscles attached like an exo-skeleton to the outside. There were air tanks on the back and pouches of food and supplies on the arms and legs. The power of the suit amplified their movements when they walked or reached. The helmets were cone-shaped, wide at the top, with a panoramic windshield served by a wiper.

The gloves, however, were made of some soft material like leather, and did not attach to the suit.

Lalcritt was driving the carrier alone this time. "You'll have to walk down that trail to get to the Wall," he said, pointing. "The Walls don't like it if we fly near them, so I won't actually go back there until that Wall breaks up in nine days or so."

"What's with the soft gloves?" Wiegand asked, speaking into a microphone built into the helmet, which drove an external speaker.

"That's what the Walls specified," Lalcritt said. He stood up from the driver's bench and turned back, his yard-wide shoulders making it an impressive maneuver.

"Are these suits always built that way?" Sani asked.

"There are no other suits," Lalcritt said. "We've never had a human on this planet before. The Hands just drew up plans for us and we made four of them."

"Still, don't the Cortay suits have sealed gloves?" Covington asked.

"I believe you have other gloves in the pack on your back," Lalcritt said. "The Hands specified that you should wear the soft gloves today. You won't be hurt — the pressure difference isn't that much, and the air is poisonous to breathe but won't hurt you otherwise. You don't want to let the gunk in the air get on your skin, but I guess the gloves will protect you from that."

"Now listen," he continued, "we can't make an anti-gravity generator small enough to fit inside a suit. Once you step outside the carrier, the suit will take you anywhere you want to walk, but you're going to sag down into it. Make sure there's no obstructions in the way of the soft parts of your body."

"Well, isn't that special," Wiegand said sourly. "You say you've never tried these out on humans before. Oh, I'm looking forward to this."

"Let's go out for a minute and we can come back in if we have to, okay?" Covington asked Lalcritt, who slowly blinked his wide-spread eyes, apparently the equivalent of a nod. They stepped into the back end of the carrier and Lalcritt closed and sealed the inner doors, then opened the back doors.

They stepped out, into more than double gravity. It was like jumping down from a tailgate: Wiegand's legs bunched up and he reeled, then caught himself and slowly stood back up. He felt heavy and his cheeks were pulled into jowls, but his suit smoothly matched the motions of his hands and legs with far more power than his own muscles could provide. The windshield wiper began to sweep as airborne drizzle and bacteria settled on it.

He turned back and helped Sani out of the carrier. Covington had stumbled and fallen, but was pulling himself erect without damage.

"How you doing, Brian?" Wiegand asked. This time, without any change of control on his part, his voice traveled by radio.

"Doin' okay," Covington said. "Or anyway, I can live with this. Can you feel, there are arch supports in the feet? The Hands thought of everything."

"These suits were made to exactly fit our bodies," Sani said. "I feel so *strong* in this!" She picked up a fallen tree trunk and waved it around.

"Yeah, yeah, the Hands are super-dupers," Wiegand said. "We should have a dance competition. I could out-dance 'em, I bet. I'd humiliate 'em."

"Even *you* could out-dance the Hands," Covington agreed solemnly, "and there are not that many entities in any universe you could say that about."

"You could out-dance me, I think," Sani said, putting down her tree trunk. "I never could dance, wasn't allowed to as a kid."

They waved to Lalcritt to indicate that they were all right, and started unsteadily down the path.

After a few minutes, they had the knack of walking with powered assistance, and could step confidently. The carrier was quickly invisible behind them.

The air was not uniformly misty. The drizzling rain and curtains of organic aerosols were swept aside by irregular winds, revealing sudden vistas of pale green valleys below them threaded with twisty silver rivers. They were on a hillside, following what might have been a game trail through a forest of trees with brittle, crackling leaves, each leaf twinkling with a little light when the tip pointed up. The sky was overcast but otherwise brighter than the sky of Brythe, except where dark wet clouds scudded across it.

Several times, they saw the overcast ahead of them open and a beam of "sunlight" arrowed down, to be met a half second later with an even brighter return stroke of photons from the ground, as quick and startling as a flashbulb. The light stormed back up to the heavens along the same straight path. The track was a line of purple dazzle in their eyes for minutes afterward.

There was running water beside them, a little streamlet that paralleled the path. "Do you suppose the rain and the creek are the same as the water-stuff on Brythe?" Wiegand asked.

"Looks like it," Sani said. "Why wouldn't it be?"

"I sure couldn't say," Covington said sadly. "None of the chemistry I know applies here to the little atoms, if they are little atoms. I kind of had the idea on Brythe that since they had that horse-and-buggy technology, I could impress them with my alien knowledge. But nothing I know is any use here."

"You obviously had a good science education back on ... on Earth," Sani said. "That's got to count for something."

"Not so much," Covington said. "It took about two minutes in Card's lab to figure out that I couldn't even get *into* a freshman chemistry class here, much less get out of it. There's physics here that we don't experience on ... you know, on the outer level, and none of the interactions between the itty-bitty atoms have any counterpart." He turned abruptly to Sani. "Church Sani," he said, "what's in the middle of a planet? Home, I mean, or Brythe. Is it dirt and rocks all the way down?"

"I don't think anybody knows, any human at least," Sani said after a pause. "We dig mines, but they don't go all that deep. Why don't you ask the Hands about it?"

"Because they'd tell me," Covington said. "Gets on my nerves after a while. What I mean is, is the surface just kind of a crust over something completely different in the middle of a planet?"

"You think the middle of the planet is nucleons doing quantum mechanical stuff, and the surface dirt is just a shell made of your itty-bitty atoms?" Wiegand asked in English.

"Yeah," Covington said.

"Cool!" Wiegand said.

"We've never found anything but rocks and dirt," Sani said. "But the Hands would know."

"You know, I'm sure the Hands are very nice people and all," Covington said, "but they're sure cramping my style as a boy scientist."

"Well, cheer up, they'll always need dishwashers," Wiegand said. "You know, Sulfur isn't as gloomy and rainy as it looked from the carrier."

"Yeah, you're right. I think it's like riding in a car in the rain," Covington said. "It always looks like the storm slacks off once you stop moving."

"This is beautiful, in its own way," Sani said. "No one ever imagined a place like this, back on Home."

Covington said, "Hey, watch where you step. We've got company." He pointed, and they could see a little file of "units" waddling through the underbrush across their path. The units' boxy armadillo bodies wobbled back and forth as they walked, their heads bobbed, and they carried their naked tails upright. One of them made a detour and scratched up the ground with its forepaw, then ate some morsel it found.

"Should we say hello?" Wiegand wondered.

"No," Covington said. "These aren't connected, so I suppose they're just rodents, or whatever an armadillo is."

"I wonder what they think about when they're animals?" Sani said. "You know, I think I understand them better as little animals than I do as big brains. They seem like perfectly nice little creatures."

"Funny to think this might have been one of the ones we talked to before," Wiegand said. "I wonder why they evolved to have that connection capability? They don't seem to do anything with their intelligence that, you know, enhances their survival or anything."

"Heck," Covington said. "Humans spend a lot of intelligence on things that don't help pass on their genes. Bible-study classes and arguing about Spiderman movies and playing Farmville doesn't have any survival value that I can see. We have a lot more brain power than we would have needed to be the top hunter-gatherers out on the savannah. I always figured that meant God is growing us for something more. I imagine He's growing the Hands, too, with more than just the brain power they need to survive."

"Why, that's standard doctrine in the church," Sani said. "That's what the Hands have always said, that we have more intelligence than we need because we use it to worship God."

"Be hard to prove something like that," Wiegand remarked.

"That's why I only say it to my friends," Covington said. "I couldn't say that in a science conference. I couldn't say it at church back home, either, the old ladies'd be all over me."

"If you said that at school, little miniature undergraduates would be all over you."

"Yeah, bless their pea-pickin' little hearts," Covington said, then continued, "Hey, here we are. It's the beast with two backs, or more like, the beast with a couple of hundred backs." They entered the meadow they had visited before and looked at the fully formed Hand of God.

It was a low wall of animals clutching each other, sprawling over an area perhaps twenty yards on a side. The units were stacked three deep, formed into curves that snaked irregularly but always left at least a couple of feet of clearance between any two sections. There were no branches: it was one continuous string.

At the head end, the electronic equipment they had left was in continuous use, flashing and winking as symbols poured across the screen. The heads of units that could turn far enough regarded the screen steadily.

Here and there, units wriggled free of the wall and were immediately replaced by others.

"Only the outer crust of a planet is made of ordinary matter," the Hand said without preamble, speaking by radio into their helmets. "The interior is very different."

"Nice to see you again, too," Covington said sourly. "Were you listening in on everything we said?"

"Of course."

"You should give us some privacy."

"Why is that?" the Hand asked.

"Um ... because we want it."

"But we want to listen," the Hand said. "When desires conflict, one must prevail. We see no harm to you from listening to your conversations, so we will continue to do it."

"But listening in when you're not invited does us harm," Wiegand said.

"Will you demonstrate this, please? We will change our opinion if we are wrong."

"Oh ... I'll get back to you," Wiegand said in frustration.

"Listen," Sani said. "Weren't you just born three days ago? How come you have all the answers now?"

"I have reached my full maturity and have entered on a life of service to God," the Hand said. "I have access to all knowledge known by other Hands, and am in continuous contact with them."

"You realize this 'life of service to God' shtick smells bad to me, and probably also to Brian although I don't think he wants to say it?" Wiegand said.

"We do realize this," the Hand said serenely. "Learning to understand your reactions is one of the reasons we have asked you to come here."

"Why did you want *me* here?" Sani demanded.

"Your presence was unplanned," the Hand said. "However, you give us an opportunity to learn more about the Inner Church movement."

Sani was silent for a moment, then said, "You weren't supposed to know about that."

"We know of and approve of it."

"What's he talking about, Church Sani?" Covington asked.

"It's a group inside the church," Sani said. "I'll tell you about it later, when we get some privacy. There is a place where we'll have some privacy, isn't there?"

"No," the Hand said.

Wiegand moved closer to it. "Did you just say there is no place to have privacy on this planet?"

"We did say that. There is no place that humans have privacy here, on Brythe or on Home."

"You ... you animals!" Sani shrieked. "You little ... why are you telling us this now?"

"Because we want you to know," the Hand said. "We can see and hear what happens in any building, anywhere that humans have settled. At this time, we wish you to learn this and communicate it to all of the people."

"They'll go crazy," Sani said. "I know it. I guess you've got some little devices planted in every building. They'll tear the buildings apart to find them."

"They will not find our devices, which are small and inconspicuous."

"Then they'll burn the buildings to ashes," Sani said.

"That will not be necessary. We will disable the listening devices and tell you exactly where they are."

"Why would anybody believe you when you say that?" Covington asked.

"Because we have never lied to you, and never will."

"You people don't understand humans at all, do you?"

"We are trying to learn," the Hand said. "That is the reason we have asked you to come to physically meet with this Hand. We can get a deeper understanding through direct neural contact. Being immobile ourselves, we have asked you to come to us rather than the other way around."

"Hoo, boy," Wiegand said. "Okay, here it comes. You have a big helmet with cables and blinkie lights you want us to put on, right? Then you take over our bodies and marry our girlfriends. We've seen this movie."

"Is Sad For Indarya your girlfriend?" the Hand asked. "We have been observing your developing relationship with interest."

"Will you stop that!"

"I apologize for any transgression," the Hand said. "In any event, we have no such plans, and no such mechanical devices. In the nature of our animal members, any unit can make neural contact directly. When informed by our intelligence, we can process information from your neural signals even though you are a different species. Will you allow us to do this? The process will not be harmful to you."

"I'll do it," Covington muttered in English to Wiegand.

"You sure you want to do this, Brian? We don't have to say yes."

"I'm good," Covington muttered, then addressed the Hand in Cortay: "You guys could learn something about a better bedside manner. But okay, I'm your guinea pig."

"You see, we did not understand the references in your reply. We would like to learn to understand all that you say," the Hand said. "We can learn much more from direct contact. Please go to the unit that is in the fourteenth column back from my head end, where you are now."

Sani said, "Sad For Brian, don't do it. I don't understand this."

"I don't think we've got much to negotiate with," Covington said. "These guys are so smart, they're ten steps ahead of us no matter what we do. I'll just do what they want, and let's hope for the best."

They walked back along the Wall, counting units until they came to the fourteenth column. The top unit was a slightly larger than normal animal, wobbling a little as it clung to the back of a smaller unit below it. As they approached, it disconnected its head from the tail of the unit ahead, and turned to look alternately at them with small unintelligent eyes.

"Please remove your glove," the Hand said by radio to Covington, "and let the unit smell your bare hand." Covington did, gingerly, then yelped and jerked his hand up. "Sumbitch bit me!" he yelled clutching his hand with the other. Blood ran over the fingers of the glove.

"It is necessary to break your skin to establish neural contact," the Hand said. "Please insert your hand into the opening on the back of this unit."

Covington was still stepping back and forth and shaking his hand. "You could have warned me!" he said.

"If we had, you would not have exposed your hand," the Hand said reasonably.

"Listen, am I going to get infected from this?"

"No. Nothing that lives on this planet you call Sulfur can live in your tissues. From the point of view of your body, this environment is sterile. Please insert your hand into the opening on the back of this unit."

"This is the 'opening' you use for sex?" Covington said. "You realize you've just pinned my creepy-meter here, right? Why do you want me to do that?"

"That is where the neural connections are. It has no sexual connotation in this situation. The unit will feel uncomfortable, but I am able to block off that sensation."

"You guys don't have much of a sense of humor, do you?" Wiegand broke in.

"We have no sense of humor," the Hand said. "It is a deficiency in us, one of several that we recognize and regret."

"All right, you comedians," Covington said. "Let's do this." He wiggled his bare, bleeding hand deep into the slot on the back of the unit. The animal placidly took the tail of the unit ahead back into its mouth and closed its eyes.

Covington stood without moving, his eyes closed. After a minute, when Wiegand was getting anxious, his eyes opened again. "It's okay," he said. "I'm all right. But this is going to take a while. Don't worry about me, but I can't really talk while I'm plugged in."

"Okay, I guess," Wiegand said.

Covington closed his eyes and was motionless again, slumped inside his red armor. Wiegand and Sani watched him for a while, but there was no further change. Presently they left to walk around idly.

Wiegand counted the number of units in the Wall and came to a total of 284, not counting the loose animals that were also loitering around the meadow, probably in an instinct-driven hope of getting lucky. He and Sani wandered down-slope and looked out at a vista of distant hills and clouds.

The forests were a palette of subtle greens and silvers under white clouds. Colors brightened and dimmed as hazy patches in the air swirled before them. There were black birds, or flying animals of some kind, wheeling in formations over the valleys.

"They're not real appealing in person, but I suppose they're perfectly okay people," Wiegand said, prompted by nothing.

"They sound a lot friendlier when you talk to them in the Hands' Chamber in the church, back home," Sani said. "I always liked to talk to them. The priest used to let me in even when he didn't have to, when I was little. One time the Hands told me stories."

"A lot of people do better remotely than in person, I guess," Wiegand said. "A lot of my friends, anyway."

"Even the Cortays are people," Sani said. "The Hands ... they're not people, not really. Do you think they really listen to everything we say?"

"Church Sani, it's sure possible. What I'm wondering is *why*?"

"Because they're envious. Because they know we're real people and they just want to be."

"Um ... maybe." Wiegand knelt and picked up a single unit that happened to be waddling by. He held it by its body in his leather-gloved hands, and the animal kicked and snapped futilely at him. It had short, thick claws on all four feet, and sharp teeth in its mouth. The ventral sex organ was recessed into a fold in the belly, and the slot on top was closed tightly. There was no anus or cloaca — apparently all elimination took place through the pores on the right side of its body.

"Maybe you could feed it a bug and make friends," Sani said.

"I don't think they have the instincts to be pets," Wiegand said. He replaced it on the ground, and the unit scurried away. "You know, that armored body sort of tells me they have enemies that they escape by hiding, and I guess they have an instinct to eat when they're hungry. Other than that, I think the only instinct is a desire to get cozy with other units when the sex urge strikes."

"They want to get connected," Sani said. "Do you think that's a clue to how the Hands think?"

"A desire to be connected?" Wiegand asked, turning the idea over in his mind. "They sure have that — from what the Cortays said, that was the first thing they wanted the Cortays to build, was a network so they could talk to each other. And God know they're all up in your business — the humans, I mean."

They turned at a squealing noise, loud enough to be audible through their helmets, voiced by dozens of units at once.

Covington was kicking the Wall to pieces. As Sani and Wiegand ran back, Covington kicked holes in the Wall in three places, the terrified units wriggling madly away from his armored boots. Covington danced back and forth in rage, grabbing units with one bloody bare hand and one gloved hand and pitching them away. The Wall was disconnected in several places, and as Wiegand watched, more units disengaged from each other and ran clumsily away.

He reached Covington, got in front of his helmet and yelled "Brian! Stop it! Chill out!"

Abruptly Covington stopped moving, and the gravity pulled him into a slump inside the suit. He paused for a few long breaths. "Yeah, I'm okay now. I just got mad," he said dully. "Let's go, let's get back to the truck thing."

"Where are we going?" Sani asked.

"Back to Brythe. There's nothing we want here anymore."

"Won't the Hands stop us? You just *killed* this one, Brian," Wiegand said.

"No, they don't think like that. Besides, they're too *good* to take revenge. They're *good* people. They're so good. God damn, they're good people."

They trudged back along the path, their mechanical muscles performing flawlessly. In the meadow, the remaining units scattered out of sight. The meadow was empty. Only the equipment was left.

Chapter 17

Leaving was not entirely Covington's decision. The Hands wanted them gone as well, and by the time the carrier returned to the Staff House, Indarya had already been bundled into her own armored suit, and all of their small store of possessions were boxed up and waiting to enter *Passenger and Cargo Craft Type 8 No. 215*, which had not been allowed to leave. Sani, Wiegand and Covington left the carrier and walked directly up the ramp into the spaceship's air lock. The three bulky suits nearly filled the small space as the door closed and the air was cycled. They walked carefully up the stairs, trying not to cause any damage with their powered limbs, and met Indarya and Vallow in the common room.

"I'm so glad to see you!" she said. Her helmet was off, giving an effect of a too-small head on an enormous body. "What happened? The Cortays came in and hustled me right out. They wouldn't tell me anything."

"They told us, the Cortays and me. Everything, you understand," Vallow said. "After that, there didn't seem to be much point in my trying to hide aboard ship."

"What?" Indarya asked, looking at their faces.

"We'd better sit down," Wiegand said. "I think they're going to take off right away."

They pulled themselves out of their red mechanical suits and stored them in lockers, then sat on the over-sized couches and tightened the seat belts. Covington sat silently, looking at nothing. The bite on his hand had stopped bleeding. "Sad For Indarya," Sani said, "you're not going to like this, but here it is. It turns out that the Hands can listen to us and I guess see us anywhere, not just in the chamber in church."

"They just started that?"

"No, I think they've always done it, or at least they've had this for a long time."

"In the toilet? In the dark?" Indarya asked.

Wiegand said, "Oh, my people have technology to see in the dark so I'm sure the Hands must have it. I think we have to assume they're watching and listening to everything, including right now."

"Everything," Indarya said uncertainly. "Everything." She suddenly gave a wild and unhumorous laugh, then stuck out her tongue and turned in her seat to give a raspberry cheer in each of four directions. "You get that, Hands?" she said. Turning to the others, she asked, "Why do they want to watch us all the time?"

"Just nosey, I think," Sani said. "Or maybe we're entertainment."

The ship took off, rising smoothly through the air. They passed above the rain clouds and the upper surface of the cloud deck was dazzling white in the light of the orbitals. They floated up through the blue sky into space.

"I know when the electron eruption will be," Covington said abruptly. "It's in about twenty-two days."

"Are you okay, Sad For Brian?" Sani asked. "You haven't said much."

"Yeah, I'm fine," he said. "I'm just ... my head is swimming. That neural-connection thing about ... it about *dissolved* me, if that makes any sense. Anyway, I learned a lot from them while they were draining me dry."

"They probably didn't expect you would be able to read them while they were reading you," Wiegand said.

"Oh, hell, they expected exactly what happened. They're so smart they're ahead of any move we could possibly make. They hold *all* the cards."

"Tell us, Sad For Brian," Sani said, leaning toward them. "Are the Hands really evil or self-centered underneath?"

"Not a bit. Of course, I have no way to prove the image they were giving me was real, but I think it was. They're good all the way through, they love God and they love us sincerely — actually, they think we're cute — and they mean us nothing but good. They've decided that humans are too dependent on the Hands and it's stifling the development of our own culture, so the loving thing to do is to break off the relationship for a generation or so. That's why they want us to spread the message that they're little connected animals, and we should tell everybody they've been snooping on us, and they've even figured out a way to use the exploding-planet crisis to help their plan, too."

"They're going to let everybody on Brythe die so that the other humans will change their opinion of the Hands?" Wiegand asked.

"Not that bad. I couldn't understand the engineering, but they're going to build a big machine on Brythe which will keep the electron from being emitted. I mean, check out the logic here. They're completely convinced this machine will work, so the people will be saved. They want *us* to get the impression they're a bunch of over-confident smart guys who are willing to risk human lives on an untested machine ..."

"Ya think?" Wiegand broke in.

"... so they're not going to arrange an evacuation. But they also know some of the Cortays will help with an evacuation once they know, and the Church can put together some funds for it, and they know about Vallow, that his people can help. So" — he held up fingers to count — "one, they know the machine will work but they want us to think it might not, and two, we'll evacuate anyway, which, three, puts the Hands in a bad light and also keeps the humans safe, so, four, they get *both* of the things they want. They want us to be safe, and they want us to dislike them. And there's not a ding-dong thing we can do about it."

Sani said, "The 'Inner Church' is a movement in the church to distance ourselves from the Hands, for exactly the reason you said. We thought the Hands didn't know about it. I wonder if we thought of that ourselves, or if the idea was planted?"

"Church Sani," Covington said earnestly, "you really *can't* out-think the Hands. If they did plant that idea, and they don't want you to find out, you'll never know."

"All right," Vallow said briskly. "The eruption is in about 22 days."

"Depends on how long the days are, of course," Covington said. "But yeah, about that."

"The flight time from my home is about ten days. Once we found out the Hands were listening to everything anyway, the Cortays let me use their communications equipment and I talked to some people back there. They're coming to get me already and we can probably get about six ships for an evacuation. Each one will hold a couple of hundred people. They'll have to pay, though. I guess we can take your local money if we're going to establish trade. Probably each ship company will want to set their own prices. Anyway, we'll need to tell your people to have cash."

"I can help with that," Sani said. "We can get the word out through the churches, and we can find some money for people that don't have it. Also, we can afford to charter a couple of Cortay ships. But are people going to believe they need to get out?"

"They will believe," said a voice from the doorway. The Cortay Captain Melchanop came in and sat down with them. "We've just gotten word from Brythe, there have been more and worse earthquakes, and the people are rioting to get away. The Hands have already told them not to worry because their machine will solve the problem, and apparently they worded the announcement so cleverly that nobody believes them."

"Thank you, sir," Indarya said. "Will the Cortays help us get away?"

"We will. We have our own church, which can arrange some ships for you, and we can probably get a few others for passengers who can pay. By the way, feel free to get up — we're done maneuvering for a while."

Wiegand stood up and began to pace around. "So we're all over this like a cheap suit," he said. "The entire planet is exploding and there's, you know, *no problem* because we've got it totally covered. Do you suppose we thought of any of this, or are the Hands just moving us around like game pieces?"

"Back 'atcha, boy scientist," Covington said. "What's the test that would distinguish one from the other? If you can't find a difference in results between explanations, then it doesn't matter which one is true."

"I don't want to live that way, that's the difference," Wiegand snapped. "If the Hands want to push us around, I'm going to push back."

"And what, get people killed on Brythe?" Covington said. "You *can't* do anything that would interfere with the evacuation, or the Hand's big machine, or anything that would put people in danger.

Pete, the Hands *win* this one. You lose, if saving all those people is a loss."

"Oh, Christ!" Wiegand yelled, and kicked at the bulkhead, which resulted in no damage at all.

"Please don't do that when you are wearing powered armor," Captain Melchanop said quietly.

"Do you think the Hands really can prevent the big explosion?" Indarya asked. "Because then we wouldn't have to leave."

"I don't have any way to judge," Covington said sympathetically. "Even when I was getting swirled away in the Hand's mind, I still only had my own brain power to use. I could see what the machine will look like, and I caught them sending out orders for a Cortay engineering team to build it, but I couldn't understand how it was supposed to work. I don't think you should take that chance. If the Hands are wrong, you'd die."

"What did the Hands learn from you?" Sani asked.

"Everything. Everything I know, and some stuff I would never have remembered on my own. They were interested in all of it."

"Do you think they understood everything?"

"I don't know," Covington said slowly. "They're smart as hell, but they don't have any ... any context, I guess is the word I want, to understand what humans think. People use sex for *everything*. We want to divide up the entire world into male and female things, we have this whole elaborate code of things you can't say to women because they sound sexual, things you have to say to women because they sound sexual, things you can't say to men for the same reason

... we spend our whole lives learning the sex code. How can somebody understand that who doesn't have sex? Not to mention not having the fear of death or the love of cooking and eating food, or for that matter scratching where it itches?"

"Brian," Wiegand said, "don't take this wrong, but I always thought it was kind of funny how you love God. God doesn't have any of that stuff either."

"But Jesus did," Covington said easily. "You need to get yourself into a church where people don't have sticks up their butts, no offense intended."

"Why, I went to a wedding in church only last year where I danced the hokey-pokey," Wiegand said. "Don't tell me white people don't know how to get funky."

In response to some unseen command from Melchanop, a Cortay crewman had appeared bringing cups of hot tea. "Guys?" Sani said, as they passed the cups around, "Exploding planet? Can we focus?"

"It can wait for a cup of tea," Vallow said. "We can't do anything until we get to Brythe anyway."

"Sad For Brian," Indarya said, "will you say grace?"

"Father God, we have so many blessings, we just thank you, Father," Covington started immediately. "We know You're watching over us with love in everything we do ..."

He prayed for minutes, until Wiegand looked up and Sani and Indarya looked down to stare at him. He prayed on and on, louder and softer, unceasing.

The others had given up and were sipping their tea long before Covington finally made his "amen."

He looked up and said, "Sorry. I needed that."

Chapter 18

New Town was a smoking wreck when the ship landed at the spaceport. It had been hit by two large and a dozen smaller earthquakes since they had left the last only hours before their arrival. They could see the tumbled buildings and fires as the ship settled. Mobs of people milled restlessly around the spaceport, held back only by hastily-erected barbed-wire fences and makeshift barricades.

"I will take a ship-load of people off immediately to the nearest human world," Captain Melchanop said, while the ship hovered a safe distance above the ground. "This ship isn't set up for passengers, but they'll be able to live in the cargo holds for a day or so. I want an orderly loading, though. Will you help me keep that crowd under control?"

"We'll do what we can," Wiegand said. "Do you have any weapons aboard this ship?"

"No, of course not. We have never needed them before. Still, if you will wear your armored suits, you should be able to handle the crowd."

"I'd still like something," Covington said. "Anything like a big stick?"

"Why, yes," the Captain said. He gestured to a crewman, who left and returned a few minutes later carrying two large wooden paddles with long handles. "Here you are," the Captain said. "We use these for spreading loose grain in the cargo hold. Will these suit you?"

Wiegand and Covington had already suited up, while Indarya and Sani were still climbing into theirs. "Power Rangers with spoons!" Wiegand said. "I like it!" He took one paddle in his armored gloves and was able to wave it around easily, even though he could barely have lifted it with his own muscles.

"Captain, how many people do you think you can carry?" Covington asked.

"I'm just going to dump all the vegetables we were carrying," the Captain said, after conferring with another officer on a communicator. "That should give us room for two hundred or so humans, a few more if some of them are children. We've got some water and some buckets for sanitary purposes, and that will have to do for a one-day voyage to Gamnon, which is the nearest human world. We'll be back if we can."

"Two hundred, okay. Ready when you are," Sani said, using her suit speaker. She and Indarya were helmeted and sealed.

"Wait in the airlock until we are on the ground," the Captain said, and left the room for the bridge. There was barely room in the airlock for the four bulky suits, and they waited with their arms at their sides while the captain emptied the cargo holds by the simple expedient of opening the cargo doors and tilting the whole ship, then leveled the ship again and settled to the ground in one of the marked landing squares. The airlock door opened.

The mob outside the spaceport fence, already excited and pressing against the gates, went mad at the sight of the ship opening. They pressed their first ranks against the barbed wire and knocked down the fences. Screaming, the fallen men, women and children at the front were trampled by the rioters running over them.

Wiegand and Covington leaped out and held their paddles at "high port," bracing for the wave of panicked humans running toward them. When the first line arrived, all fast-running men, they smacked them back with sweeping strokes of the paddles.

A group got behind Wiegand and knocked him down by kicking at the back of his knees. He fell forward, unhurt inside the suit but losing his grip on his paddle. A band of men carried the paddle away while others rolled him over with kicks to keep him off balance.

Indarya, huge and terrifying in her armor, ran to his aid. She leaped over Wiegand, landed in the middle of the crowd and ran down the group with the paddle. She wrested it away from them and swung it in a circle over her head. The rioters fell over themselves to get away.

In the meantime, three men had reached the airlock door. Sani reached inside with one arm, picked them up by the shirt fronts and flung them back, then closed the door.

Sani took off her helmet and dropped it on the ground. Her head looked tiny and vulnerable in the center of the big neck collar. She strode forward and shouted, and her words were amplified by the suit into an awesome roar. "I AM CHURCH SANI!" she yelled. "I SPEAK FOR THE CHURCH!"

The sound was stunning. In concentric circles around her, the crowd was cowed to silence. Wiegand rolled over and lumbered to his feet, and Indarya gave him back the paddle. He and Covington retreated to either side of the airlock door, their backs protected by the ship, and held their paddles out. Sani walked a few steps farther forward, and her voice was still tremendously amplified even though she was no longer shouting.

"I am Church Sani," she said again. Echoes came back from the nearby hillsides. "God knows the suffering you have endured, the Hands know it, the Church knows it and I know it. God speaks to you in your heart, the Hands speak for themselves and I can tell you that the Church is bringing ships to take you safely away, right now. This ship is only one of many. Everyone will be rescued."

A loudmouth in the crowd started to argue with her. Indarya strode through the mob, her red powered suit creating a bow wave of retreat, picked him up with both hands and held him overhead. She put him down when he quieted.

Sani surveyed them all with scorn. "This ship will carry the sick, the injured and families with small children. You know that, you knew it all along, and yet you panicked and ran to get here over the bodies of others.

"So here is how it's going to be. Clear off a space around this door. Bring us the injured on litters, and the sick and injured who can walk. If you try to fool us, you will regret it, and I don't mean that you will feel remorse, I mean that we will beat you ourselves. When all of the casualties and medical caregivers are aboard, we will fill up the remaining space with families with children."

She replaced her helmet, and ceased to be a small haranguing woman and became a faceless huge robot again. "Sad For Brian, Sad For Pete," she said over the radio, "Close the cargo door for a minute and let's make some space here."

Covington and Wiegand advanced again with their wooden paddles, this time close together and guarding each other's back. A few men and women tried to run past them and were batted back, and then the crowd melted away from them.

A nurse Sani knew personally had forced her way to the front of the crowd. She and Sani picked out a couple of others with medic training. Presently they had a line organized and were inspecting patients brought to them on makeshift litters of blankets and poles. All passed inspection except one, and were carried into the ship. The one imposter was hoisted overhead by Sani and thrown, wailing, into the crowd.

Families with children lined up next. Indarya took off her helmet briefly to glare at one couple clutching a squirming boy she happened to know was not theirs. They turned and ran, and the boy got away from them.

Presently the ship was full. They banged on the hull, and Vallow came out, looking small and vulnerable next to the four suits of armor. They closed the door, and with no more ceremony than that the Captain lifted his ship up into the sky. The crowd was not visibly smaller than it had been. They followed the ship with upturned heads until it vanished, then turned back to look at the five outsiders.

"Let's form up into a square," Covington said, on both the radio and outside speaker. "Vallow, you get in the middle. March slow but don't stop for anybody. I don't know where to go, though."

"I need to meet with the church," Sani said. "The main church might still be standing. Anyway, it's a direction."

"Okay," Covington said. "Over the bridge and into town."

The crowd was concentrated at the bridge leading into town, but they gave way reluctantly to the overwhelming force of the four suits of powered armor. Vallow paced nervously in the center, unwilling to look left or right, while Covington and Wiegand swept the mob back with their wooden paddles. On the far side of the bridge, the crowd thinned out and they marched through the tumbled, smoking ruins of houses and shops. Indarya pointed to a crowded scene that had been a small park.

"I think they've got kind of a field hospital set up," she said. "If you folks don't need me, I think I'll go help out there."

"I guess we'll be okay going into town," Sani said. "Vallow, you'll come with us to talk to the church, right?"

"I will," Vallow said, "but slow down, will you? I can't keep up with those suits."

"Do you want me to carry you?" she asked.

Vallow looked nonplussed for a moment, then grinned and said, "Yes!" Sani knelt down and he climbed on her shoulders, then waved as she stood up.

"I don't need to talk to the church either," Wiegand said. "I'll stay here with Sad For Indarya and help out. They might need guards, that crowd at the spaceport looks restless."

"Good enough," Covington said. "We'll call you on the radio if these radios have enough range."

"Oh, cripes, the kind of engineering the Hands do, you could probably call back to Sulfur with these suits. Actually, I suppose the Hands are listening now."

"Most likely," Covington said.

Sani was staring in the direction of the town center. There was another mob of hundreds of men and women, traveling toward the spaceport, milling and yelling. The mob would miss their present position by a few hundred yards.

"Who's the guy at the head of that parade?" she asked. "I can't place him but I think I know him."

"We know him," Wiegand said. "That's Card. Gron Orrata Hemmet Card, I mean. He's *leading* that mob."

"Sure as hell," Covington said. "He's walking pretty fast for a pudgy guy. What's going on?"

"He's going to miss the hospital," Indarya said. "I think we should let him go. We don't want them coming here."

"Yeah," Covington said. "Okay, we can move pretty fast in these suits. Vallow, can you hang on tight there? Then let's get a move on."

Covington and Sani began to run, with Vallow bouncing on her shoulders.

"They need us over at the hospital, I think," Indarya said. "Better take off our helmets so we don't look so scary."

"Card looks like he's got a lynch mob," Wiegand said, staring after them. "I think I'd better be ready to look scary again."

"Don't worry about him right now."

Chapter 19

New Town had never been large enough to have more than a tiny hospital and a few doctors. Now what medical force they had had was completely overwhelmed by the casualties of the latest earthquake. In the open space of a park near the edge of town, volunteers had set up sloppy, flapping tents and a few big pots of dubiously clean water. The area outside of the tents was covered with makeshift beds and litters, many of them made from the doors of fallen houses. Some of the injured were silent and apathetic. Others screamed and thrashed.

There were a few startled looks at the big powered suits, but Indarya and Wiegand quickly made themselves useful by hoisting away piles of debris. When they had the area fairly well policed, one of the women there who seemed to know Indarya banged on her armor to get her attention, then pointed to an area off to one side.

"Sad For Pete," she said, "I'm going to take over where they have the babies. The women there are beat and need to rest."

"I'll go with you," he said. They walked over to a section of hastily-built trestle tables. Two of them were filled with tiny squalling babies, and another was used for changing diapers. A reeking pile of soiled diapers lay nearby.

Indarya conferred with the women there, who were clearly exhausted, then slid out of her powered suit. They found a hat for her, which was too large and, in Wiegand's opinion, made her look cute. She started changing babies. She pointed to the diapers and asked Wiegand, "Will you do me a favor and go rinse those out at the river? You might want to put your helmet back on, or at least get a hat somewhere."

"Okay," Wiegand said. "Which way is the river?"

"Go that way, downstream a little. You don't want to get in the way of anybody's drinking water."

"Got it." Wiegand replaced his helmet, grateful for the stored air supply, and scooped up the diapers in his gloved hands. He trotted down to the river bank, ignoring the stares of passers-by, waded out into the deeper water and vigorously rinsed each diaper, as well as fastidiously rinsing his suit. When he returned, he spread the diapers out on the ground to dry.

Indarya had caught up on diaper-changing and was now cutting vegetables with a kitchen knife. She minced up the vegetables, added some meat from a can and put it all into a hand-operated grinder to reduce it to paste. As Wiegand watched, she picked up one crying baby, cuddled and soothed it until it was quiet, then let it suck gobbets of the paste from her fingers.

"Indarya," Wiegand began.

"Sad For Indarya," she said absently, then looked around. "Well, maybe not. Maybe I am just Indarya. Anyway, thanks for getting the diapers. There's some more over there."

"Sad For Indarya, what are you feeding those babies? They look like newborns or maybe preemies."

"They are newborns, some of them just today. I'm feeding them food, of course. What else would they eat? There you go, sweetheart, now you lay down and sleep for a while." She put down the baby and picked up the next one.

Wiegand tried to think of the word for "milk" and couldn't find it. "A fluid that the mother produces," he finally said.

"That's disgusting! Who would do that? Besides, there's no nutrition in urine."

"How does a mother feed babies usually?" Wiegand asked.

Indarya looked at him. "Sad For Pete, you ask the *oddest* questions. A mother chews up food and kisses the baby to give it to him, which is how they bond together. We only do it this way when the baby's not yours. Most of these poor little angels don't have mothers, or the mothers are missing still. Some of these eggs were found on the *ground*, for God's sake."

"Women lay *eggs*?"

"You know, Sad For Pete, I sometimes have to tell guys how to behave themselves. I don't usually have to tell them where babies come from." She finished feeding the baby and picked up another.

"But, but," Wiegand sputtered. "If women lay eggs and don't give milk, why do women have breasts?" He pointed.

Indarya grinned. "Why ask?" she said. "With a smooth line like that, you're not likely to get a sniff anyway, are you?"

"A sniff?"

"Sad For Pete, ask me some other time and I'll explain the facts of life to you. Really, I will. Right now, go rinse out more diapers, will you? I can't ask anybody else."

* * *

The big church in the center of New Town had been built solidly of brick and survived with little damage, although wooden buildings were flattened around it. The fires had also spared the area. When Covington, Sani and Vallow arrived, they found a group already assembled in the sanctuary.

The priest they had talked to, God Nahallit, was there, along with a couple of other men wearing the distinctive hats. There were twenty or thirty other men and women, wearing variations on a costume of knitted sweaters and tights which was different from the styles worn on Brythe. Some of them greeted Sani by name. She quickly went to confer with them, while Covington removed his powered suit and was given a baggy hat by a man in Brythean dress. He and Vallow waited uncertainly at one side.

"You know," Covington said to Vallow in a low voice, "I'm getting used to this place pretty fast. This already looks like 'church' to me."

"Churches on my world are different," Vallow said, "and I'm not much of a church-goer anyway. All I can think is that all of this will be destroyed."

"Nothing will stand if that electron emission goes off," Covington agreed. "All you can do is not be there when it happens."

Sani came back, and spoke loudly for the benefit of all. "Sad For Brian, Sad For Vallow, this is a meeting of the Inner Church. Some of them live here on Brythe, some of them just traveled here from Home to help us and to decide what to do. We all have a modern viewpoint, are willing to learn the truth about the Hands or anything else, and we can communicate with the Inner Church and the regular church hierarchy on Home.

"Everyone, this is Sad For Brian and Sad For Vallow. Both of them have come from other worlds. Sad For Brian's story is especially strange. The Hands know all about them, and as you know by now, the Hands also know all about us. Sad For Brian can tell us about what is happening on Brythe, and Sad For Vallow can help us with the evacuation. Please hear them out. Sad For Brian, will you start?"

Covington stepped forward, looked at all the church folk in front of him, and said, "Giving thanks and praise to God, who is the center of my life, I'm Brian Covington and I bring you greetings from Portal of Praise Church at 1100 West 117th Place, Chicago, Illinois, and pastor James Wardell."

They looked at him blankly. Covington stopped in confusion, then muttered "Sorry. That just kind of slipped out." He stopped a moment to collect himself, then started over.

"I'm Brian Covington," he said, "and I am from a planet you haven't heard of called Earth. Later on I'll tell you my whole story, which is kind of complicated. Right now I just want to say that I have been to visit the Hands on their planet, and between what they told me and what I know from my own world, I know some things about what's happening on Brythe. The earthquakes are related to a tremendous explosion called an electron emission, and the Hands say it will happen in about ... um ... eighteen days, more or less."

"Can we trust that deadline?" someone called out. "Are the Hands telling the truth?"

"We don't have any possible way to know," Covington said. A murmur ran through the group and he thought that perhaps their "modern viewpoint" didn't run all that deep. "The one thing we can be sure of is that we need to get people evacuated right away. If we're ahead of time, it won't matter much. If we're late it'll be a tragedy."

"And what happens," God Nanhallit asked, "if we evacuate everybody and then nothing happens? This planet is home to the people who live here, or at least some of them. They won't forgive being uprooted for nothing. Not to mention all the wealth that would be lost on Home."

"Let me tell you about big explosions," Covington said. "We have some experience on my planet." He paced back and forth, gesticulating and pleading, the perfect speaker for a "Come-to-Jesus meeting". First he explained his calculations of the size of the electron that would be emitted, with help from Sani to put it into the local terms of measurement.

He told them about the shock wave that would raise mountains and cross continents, about the dust clouds that would not clear for years, about "nuclear winter" that would destroy most of the plants and with them, all of the food.

"My planet used to be full of ... well, of species of big animals before they were wiped out by an incoming rock that wasn't a tenth of the size this outgoing rock is going to be. People, don't think you can ride this out. Anybody who is still on Brythe when that emission takes place will be dead, dead, dead a day later."

Vallow had brought up a chair, and Covington gratefully collapsed into it.

"How about the machine the Hands say they're building? Will that work to prevent this?" another voice called out.

"It might," Covington said. "I think the Hands believe it will work. They want *us* to be dubious about it because they've decided we put too much reliance on them. *I* think we should be dubious about them because ... because I'm dubious, I guess. The Hands are damn fine engineers but they only learned about this electron emission in the last few days, they're building the machine without a single chance to test it, I don't understand the principle of it and I can't tell you whether they really do or not, and the Hands don't even have hands themselves, they have to work though the Cortays to build the thing. They're playing a game to see which of us will give in to fear. On Earth we call it 'playing chicken' — I don't know what you say here. The Hands want us to evacuate even if the machine works perfectly."

"Will the Hands help with the evacuation?"

"No. That's part of their strategy of spreading the message, 'You can't trust the Hands.'"

"We'll get some help from the Cortays," Sani put in, "and you should listen to Sad For Vallow, also. But we'll still have to arrange at least some ships from Home, and find a way to pay for them."

God Nanhallit stood up in the front row. He turned back to address the others. "I know a little more about Sad For Brian's story," he said, "and I have learned that the Hands believe it, so I believe it too. But Sad For Brian" — he turned back — "your world really has no experience with an event like this, and I think that most of what the Hands know is what they learned from you. If we evacuate everybody off this planet, people will never return here even if the explosion never happens. Twenty thousand people will lose their homes and their jobs and have to live as refugees. I agree we don't want to take a chance on getting caught by an explosion, but can't you give us more assurance that this is really leading up to an explosion?"

Another man stood up in the back. "I'm Sad For Rallion," he said, "and most of you know me. I'm a worshipper of God and a member of the Inner Church, but I'm also the man who owns three factories on this planet. Look, if there's really going to be an explosion, then we have to evacuate everybody. Nobody's arguing we should risk people's lives. But I wish I could be sure you're not throwing away my life's work rather than make a hard decision."

"If we evacuate," Covington said, "and then it turns out the Hand's machine works, I guess everybody could come back."

"And everything would be just the way we left it?" Rallion asked. "It doesn't work that way. You can't take apart a planet society and put it back together again like a kid's toy."

"And anyway," a woman said from somewhere, "where are we going to get enough ships? It takes three days and a lot of money to make a round trip anywhere, and each ship only holds, what, a hundred people? Two hundred?"

Vallow stepped forward. "I should speak," he said. "My name is Vallow and I am a trader from a planet that, so far, the Hands have never permitted the Cortays to reach. I came here to establish a trading station, but I wrecked my ship and have had to ask the Cortays to communicate with my home. Just like my friend Sad For Brian, there's more to tell and I'll share it with you later. Right now I want to say that I talked with people from my planet this morning, using the Cortay's communicator, and they will send at least nine ships. These are privately owned and they will charge your people for the trip, but of course saving your lives will be worth the cost. The ships should be here in about two more days."

A man stood up at the back of the sanctuary. "Excuse me," he said. "Sad For Vallow, I've got a message for you. I'm part of the staff at the spaceport. They just got word from the Cortays that there's another ship approaching Brythe, one they can't identify. They say it must be one of your people's."

"That's impossible!" Vallow said. "There hasn't been time to get a ship here since I sent out the message."

"That's what they told me," the man said.

"It's not one of ours," Vallow said positively. "Somebody else must have heard that message I sent."

* * *

Wiegand gathered the diapers and left. Later, there was other and more grim work for him. He put the powered suit to use digging graves, carrying bodies, filling buckets of clean water. Another, smaller Cortay spaceship came into port and volunteered to carry out a hundred refugees. Wiegand led a party carrying litters with injured men and women down to the ship, parting the still-seething mob around the spaceport with his wooden paddle.

Gron Orrata Hemmet Card was still there, standing on a box and orating urgently to a crowd around him. Wiegand looked, but did not stop to listen before he returned to Indarya.

She was still busy feeding and changing her orphan babies — a few had been added to the table while Wiegand was gone. Another woman had appeared to help her, and they both gave a quick greeting to Wiegand.

Night fell unexpectedly, as it always did (at least for Wiegand), and in the manner of the humans of this world, the babies fell immediately asleep and neither got nor needed any other care. Indarya lay on the ground, rolled in a blanket. Wiegand found it was just as comfortable to sleep in his suit and merely lay down, facing upward.

That night, for the first time since his first night on Brythe, he was wakeful. He opened his eyes to see a procession of the hamburger-bun Cortay spaceships gliding overhead, heading for the spaceport. There were at least two dozen of them, one after another. He sat up to see better.

The ships landed two at a time in the spaceport. Large cargo containers were quickly off-loaded by

Cortay crews, and the ships floated immediately back into the sky and were gone. They did not take on refugees.

In a short time the ships had all left, and Wiegand could see artificial lights, brighter than the human's spear-point lamps, flaring at a camp just outside of the spaceport fence.

He could not stay awake longer. There was another ground tremor during the night, but neither Wiegand nor most of the others woke for it. Morning did not come for a long time.

Chapter 20

In the first light of morning, the ground around the spaceport was littered with the sleeping bodies of the previous day's mob. They awoke to two new sights.

The first was a new spaceship which had arrived silently during the night, of a kind no one had seen before. It was a cube, painted white with a bold design of stripes and strange lettering in dark green. It was larger than a house, but overall a little smaller than the usual Cortay ships. It had cargo ports on the ground level which were open. Human crewmen, fierce men with plaited hair and no hats, were already up and working around it.

The second new thing was the bustling Cortay work camp just outside the fence on the side away from New Town. They had circled themselves with their own fence to make an area half the size of the spaceport, ringed with cargo containers, anti-gravity lifters of a dozen kinds, and tents for living quarters and workrooms. At least a hundred Cortays were working there, building a massive project in the center. Already the metal framework was higher than the spaceport buildings. The tops of the girders sparkled with light.

The crew of the new spaceship brought out power saws and summarily cut the spaceport fence down. Sections of the fence fell inward, and with enthusiastic gestures the crewmen smiled and waved for the people to come aboard. A squad of crewmen with weapons trotted out to keep away the spaceport guards.

Sleepy and blinking, but with a dawning hope, the people stumbled tentatively forward, then walked, then ran to the ship. Some tried to ask questions, but it quickly developed that the crew of the ship did not speak their language. Others in the crowd took the opportunity and rushed to the cargo doors.

There were guards at the cargo doors. They accepted some, turned others away, and still the crowd pressed forward.

Away from the ship, there was a commotion at the bridge over the river. People and horse-carts scattered away in all directions as Covington and Sani, massive and mechanical in their powered suits, came running down the street from town. Vallow was mounted on Covington's shoulders, holding on desperately. They pounded over the bridge and across the fallen fence, then stopped for Vallow to dismount. He stared at the ship, breathing hard.

"You know these guys?" Covington said, using the outside speaker.

"They're from my world, all right," Vallow said, still catching his breath. "I've heard of this company, I think. Don't know anything much about them. They sure aren't part of the group I talked to." He yelled a greeting to a nearby crewman, who looked at him in amazement and went to confer with another, without answering.

"You think they were just cruising nearer than the others?" Covington asked.

"Must be. But what were they doing?"

"Sad For Brian," Sani said tightly, "they're turning away a lot of people."

"They're not here for a rescue, I think," Vallow said.

"You think they're only taking people who can pay?" Covington asked.

"I think they're only taking healthy men and girls," Sani said. "I think they're only taking the people they want."

"You think they're slavers or something?" Covington asked.

"And traffickers. Some of those girls are young."

"Could be," Vallow said. "We have legal indentured labor — you know, the kind of thing where you never get out of debt — and these guys could be mixed up in that, or worse."

"Pete, Sad For Indarya," Covington said. The suit switched his voice to radio without command. "Can you put your suits on and get down to the port? We've got a problem here."

"I'm already suited up," Wiegand said over the radio. "I'll get Indarya. Give us a few minutes. What's up?"

"Tell you when you get here. Make it fast," Covington said. To the others he said quietly, "Let's break this up." The suit put his voice on the outside speaker. He turned and yelled with tremendous amplification at the crowd, "Get back! Get away! This ship may not be good! Back off!"

The people in the crowd, already spooked by the sight of the powered suits and by the increasingly grim look of the crewmen, took fright and ran. Amid the confusion, one of the crewmen raised a weapon, aimed at Vallow and fired. Vallow was hit in the leg. He spun into the air and flopped to the ground, screaming, his leg instantly red with blood. Sani charged the crewman and batted him to the ground with one sweep of her suit's arm. She stepped on his gun and broke it.

Instantly the remaining crewmen closed the cargo door on the refugees they already had. The ones closest to the remaining door sprinted for it with no attempt to cover for their more distant mates. The ship began to lift.

Covington ran for the ship and leaped for the still-closing door. A crewman kicked at his hands, and Covington convulsively grabbed him by the ankle. The crewman was flung through the air wailing. Covington still had one hand on the door frame, and with the aid of the suit's power was able to pull himself aboard. The ground receded quickly below him.

A shot cracked the glass of his helmet, whining past his ear. Covington could barely see through the crazed glass. He leaped forward and grabbed for his attacker's gun, but misjudged. His armored hand grabbed the man's chest instead and crushed out a fatal wound. The man fell, instantly dead.

Covington scrambled forward and the outer and inner airlock doors closed behind him. He pulled off his helmet and tossed it away. He was on what was clearly the bridge of the ship. It was deserted. As he watched, the door on the far side closed as the remaining crewmen hid from him.

There was a bewilderingly crowded bank of computer screens, switches, lights and other controls below a broad window. Outside, the horizon was tilting as the ship wobbled out of control.

"Hands!" Covington yelled. "I know you're tracking me. This is your problem too. Help me!"

"Take the rectangular plate that is slightly above the counter top and hold it in both hands," a calm voice said in his ear. "Turn it slightly to the left. Now watch the screen directly in front of you, and straighten the plate when the green column rises to the top bar."

The ship gradually leveled. It was traveling at a tremendous rate of speed, far faster than the Cortay ships had moved. The artificial gravity compensated perfectly and kept his weight at what would be normal for a carbon-nucleus, size twelve world: he felt a little lighter than usual. "Okay so far," Covington said into the air. "How do we get back?"

"There is a situation you must handle first," the Hands said. "There is an automatic pilot you can set. Press the red button to your upper left, then slide the center four slide switches to the middle position in the bank below that button." Covington did this and stepped back. The ship continued as before.

"The remaining crewmen are taking the refugees hostage to force you to give up control," the Hands said without emotion. "We have no presence in this ship except sensors in your suit. You must defeat them."

"You're going to tell me how, right?"

"We have no expertise in this area. You will know better than we do what to do."

"That's the first time I've ever heard you guys say that," Covington remarked. "How did you know how to work this ship?"

"We have had contact with this culture before."

"How do you know about this hostage thing if you don't have any sensors here?"

"There is a camera in the hold which displays on the control board in front of you. Look to the upper right."

"Oh, damn. Damn." Covington looked at the video display and saw crewmen with guns rounding up the people they had taken aboard and tying them with ropes. "Jesus, help me now," he said aloud, and to the Hands, "Is there some clever way I can cut off their air or something like that?"

"Not from the inside," the Hands said.

"Is there another door into the hold?"

"No."

"Fat lot of help you guys are. Look, can I get at them from outside?"

"Your helmet is cracked, and there are no other spacesuits here. You would die from lack of air."

Covington looked at his helmet on the deck. The glass was cracked but still in the frame. There were two small holes, one in the glass where the bullet entered and another where the bullet burst out of the back of the helmet. He suddenly realized how narrowly he had escaped death, and began to shake. It was minutes before he could function again.

Finally Covington shook his head to clear it and asked, "How many crewmen are in there?"

"We have seen four on the screen."

"So my strategy is to run in real fast and take out at least four guys with guns without getting shot in the head? That's your advice? Strategy like that I could think up myself."

"We have not offered any advice," the Hands said.

"Come to think of it, you haven't. Are there any weapons here on the bridge?"

"Not that we know of."

"Terrific. You had this all planned out, right?"

"No," the Hand said. "We are intelligent but not omniscient."

The sound that went with the video picture of the hold suddenly came on. "Hey, man with the armor," a girl with a crewman's gun pointed at her head said. "I think they're going to kill us if you don't let them back into the bridge. Please!"

"Yeah, yeah, I'm on it," Covington muttered, and then had a thought inspired by the imminence of death by bullets. "Hey, Hands, I need some duct tape," he said. "Is there anything like that here?"

"Please explain."

"Heavy-duty sticky sheets of something, for repairs."

"There may be strips like that in the utility locker behind you," the Hands said. "Repair and maintenance supplies are stored there."

Covington opened the locker. Whatever their moral character, the alien humans were good sailors. The locker was neat, well-organized and fully stocked. He found strips of thin pliable metal with adhesive, suitable for patching a spacesuit or, he supposed, a small breach in the hull. He also found and took a tube of glue and two coils of rope.

Covington patched the helmet with the sticky strips. On the back he pasted two of them in an "X" pattern over the bullet hole, then shrugged and added a third patch on top of those.

On the faceplate, he smeared the cracks with glue and smoothed the strips over the hole while trying to leave as much clear glass as possible. When he put the helmet on, he could see nothing with his right eye, but there was an unbroken patch the size of a coin available to his left eye. He bumped into the console trying to turn around.

"Okay, let's try this," he said to the Hands. "There's something I can do from outside, right?"

"Those patches may not hold," the Hands said. "You may die."

"You guys aren't much for recovering when plans go wrong, are you?"

"Plans should not go wrong. Plans should account for all possibilities."

"Right. I'm going to go outside, and you tell me what to do, okay?"

The sound came back again on the video screen. Covington looked up and saw a crewman pointing a gun at the head of a terrified, rope-bound man. As he watched, the crewman pulled the trigger, then tossed the dead body away with contempt. The message was unmistakable.

"Oh, my God," Covington said softly, then, "Hands! Tell me how to cycle through the airlock."

He entered the airlock, closed the inner door and followed the Hands' directions to vent the air and open the outer door. He carefully knotted the rope to a knob on his suit, and to a metal ring outside the airlock door, going back to his Boy Scout days to ensure that he tied a square knot and not a granny. He pulled himself around to the outer surface of the cubical ship, weightless now.

As long as he looked at the prosaic, painted surface of the ship (riveted steel, or whatever the local equivalent was), he was fine. The white hull with green-paint trim was reassuring and soothing, even though his view was limited to the one fragment of clear glass before his left eye, surrounded by fractured craziness. From his perspective an inch away, he could even see brush marks in the paint, a homely touch. The light was like daylight on a bright, cloudy day.

"Work your way to your right. There are hand-holds and tie points on the hull," the Hand said.

Covington tied his second rope to the next loop to the next ring, untied the first rope and pulled himself to the right. A few repetitions of this technique brought him to the right-angle corner of the hull, his faceplate still nearly touching the metal. He noted a tiny hiss of escaping air from some crack in the helmet and wondered how long he could hold out.

He tied his forward rope to a ring on the next face of the cube, around the corner, but pulled too hard to release the trailing rope. He swung back-first out at the end of the forward rope. He twisted and flailed. The little spot of clear glass in front of his left eye was presented with a view of the whole universe.

He was far above the level in which the Cortay ship had traveled. He was in "outer space", still surrounded by the atoms that made up the protein but outside of its molecular orbital.

It was so beautiful that he was dumb-struck with fear.

The space around Earth is *empty* — the stars, the planets, all of the rocks and inclusions present themselves as nothing more than dots. The moon and the sun are circles, but they clearly are small objects floating in the void themselves. Covington had thought that he understood the emptiness of space from looking up at the dozen stars visible from a street in Chicago on a clear night.

The universe around him now was not empty at all. There were black patches, without stars or any gleam of light, which looked outside of the protein. The view in those directions was as vasty and hostile as the space he was familiar with.

All of the electrons in all of the five thousand atoms of the protein molecule merged together to form the molecular orbital. Covington saw it as columns and rooms and arches of misty white light. But the rooms were big enough to hold a solar system, even though Covington could turn his one usable eye from top to bottom, from left to right and take in the whole structure. On the far sides of the structure he was in, he could see receding vistas of more white structure framing black windows.

It was like an ivory puzzle ball, intricacies inside of intricacy. It was like a house of mirrors, like an M.C. Escher drawing, like lying on the rug as a little kid at Christmas time, looking up into the endless bright branching of the Christmas tree.

Covington thought he could have handled emptiness, but this left him cringing with agoraphobia, clutching his rope as he bounced gently from the hull and swung back the other way. He squeezed his eyes shut.

"Go three more rings to the right," the Hands chanted with machine-like patience. "Go three more rings to the right. Go to the right. Tie your rope to the next ring on the right and untie the rope from the ring on your left. Go to the right." Eventually it got through to Covington's shocked consciousness, and he breathed deeply, then clumsily pulled himself back to the hull and tied the rope to the next ring.

Presently he was facing a rectangular panel. "Open the panel by pressing one finger into each of the two holes at the bottom," the Hands said. The panel floated free, and having no way to hold on to it, Covington just flung it away, banging himself into the hull again in reaction.

"Okay," he said shakily. The recess in the hull held a number of connector sockets, possibly for the equivalent of electricity (Covington reflected ruefully on his continuing ignorance) and data. There was also a bank of buttons, sliders and other controls. "You're going to tell me why I'm doing this, right?" he asked the Hand.

"Some of these controls deal with the artificial gravity inside," the Hands said. "You can set up a fluctuating pattern that will disturb everyone inside and possibly allow you to overcome the crewmen."

"As plans go, that's not much better than the last one."

"It is all we can offer."

"I suppose so. Okay, tell me what to do here." Covington worked the controls according to the Hands' directions, then slowly worked his way left back to the airlock. He paused to turn outward for one more look at the sky, so crowded with electron clouds and so terrifyingly empty.

"Be careful going in," the Hand said. "The fluctuating gravity will affect you also."

Covington thought a silent prayer as he tapped the door control, then pulled himself aboard. The outer door sealed behind him, the inner door opened, and he was tumbled forward to land with a clatter on the deck as a surge of gravity caught him.

He pulled himself to his knees and suddenly sailed up to crash into the ceiling as the gravity switched off. A moment later he fell again to the deck. The gravity washed him from side to side also, as well as bouncing him up and down.

The powered suit was a dangerous hindrance to him now. Every panicky movement he made was amplified tremendously. He had thrown himself into the walls and the console several times before he was able to crawl out of the suit. He held tightly to the edge of the control console and tried to calm down. Then he vomited helplessly.

His only advantage was that the others had been subjected to this nauseation for several minutes longer. Covington staggered to his feet, grabbed the heavy powered suit and dragged it to the bulkhead door. He pulled the suit to one side, opened the door and tossed the suit in ahead of him.

It caught a crewman standing inside the door with a gun. The crewman was knocked down, and Covington landed on him heavily, grabbed his head as a surge pulled them down and banged the man's head on the deck. The crewman was knocked insensible, but Covington was racked with pain where he had landed on an elbow. He gasped for breath, then vomited again.

He reached a second door at the end of the corridor and opened it into the cargo hold. The stench was terrible — obviously all the refugees had had the same reaction to the madly shifting gravity. They were sprawled in every possible posture across the floor of the hold. Covington intended to look around and plan out an attack, but a wave of gravity lifted him and tossed him down a ramp into the hold. The powered suit rolled after him.

He landed near another crewman, a huge, strongly-muscled man, the front of whose clothing was completely fouled with vomit. Covington crawled toward him and tried to scream menacingly. However, the man had no fight left in him. He moaned and tried to rise to face Covington, but his weapon was on the floor and Covington grabbed it and beat him clumsily in the face with the butt of it. The crewman fell.

The weapon was ruined by the banging it had taken but used as a club, it was the best option Covington had. He carried it with him as he stood up and looked for the other crewmen.

One of them found him first. The noise of a shot crashed through the hold and a bullet bounced ringingly off the wall behind Covington. The sound seemed to come from all around, but he located the crewman with painful slowness and tied to run toward him. A gravity surge tumbled Covington into the lap of a man on the deck.

"I'm all tied up," the man said. "Can you throw me?"

"Um, yeah," Covington said. "You going to be okay?"

"Don't ask silly questions."

The gravity happened to drop to a few percent of normal. Covington grabbed the bound man and threw him through the air at the crewman. The crewman had his weapon up and fired, but it hit the soaring man in the ankles and made his body spin wildly as he slammed into the crewman. The rifle went flying. Covington leaped forward and cracked the crewman with his rifle butt, knocking him out.

Abruptly the gravity fluctuations ceased. Apparently the Hands had set a time limit on their manipulations. Covington stood in the restabilized gravity, reeling, and turned around just in time to see one last crewman aim his weapon and fire.

The shot went through his right shoulder. Covington cried out and fell in a blaze of pain, unconscious.

He awoke where he had fallen. The wound in his shoulder was still bleeding, but with a quick "Thank you, Jesus!" he realized the bullet had not struck an artery.

"Can you help me?" a woman behind him said. "Can you get me untied?"

"I'm hit," Covington said, instantly indignant.

"Everybody else is tied up," she said. "You're the only one with your hands free."

"I can't move my hand," Covington said.

"That guy with the gun left," she said. "If you can't, you can't, but we might not get any other chance."

"Oh, Jesus!" Covington said with no reverence at all, but tried to roll over. The pain knocked him out again, but when he recovered he was lying on his brightly painful right side (bleeding more freely now), with his left hand free. He could see the woman now, tied at the ankles and with her hands tied behind her. She wriggled over until her hands were close to him.

Covington wanted nothing more than to close his eyes and be miserable, but he reached out his left hand and began pulling at the knot. He had very little strength or control, but eventually he worked a loop free, then pulled out an end, then loosened the knot completely. The woman quickly sat up and untied her ankles, then pulled off her soft cap and ripped a strip from her shirt, and bound up Covington's shoulder as well as she could. He lapsed back into unconsciousness without another word.

He awoke to find himself on a pile of tarpaulins, obviously put together to make a bed. A man was tending him, and a glance showed him that his wound had been re-dressed with other rags, but in a more professional way. "I'm a medical start-man," the man said as soon as he saw Covington's eyes open. "We're taking care of you."

"Thanks," Covington said. "What's going on?"

"That last pirate is up on the bridge with the door locked," the medic said. "The other ones that are still alive are tied up. But we can't get up there and he's not coming out."

Covington tried to lift his head and didn't get very far. He did manage to see a knot of people standing to one side. Obviously they had all untied one another and were having some kind of discussion. "What's going on there?" he asked.

"They're having a conversation with that red suit of armor you were wearing," the man said. "You get some rest now."

Covington groaned in frustration but could not get up. He sank into an uneasy rest for a few minutes, until a young woman approached, conferred with the "medical start-man" for a moment and then shook him awake by his good shoulder. "Sad For Brian?" she asked. Covington nodded.

"We've been talking with the Hands of God through that suit of yours. They tell us it's locked so that only you can wear it."

"Is it?" Covington asked.

"That's what they say. We need to use that suit, so the Hands want to know if you can move enough to get into it."

Covington swore inexpertly for a full minute, but then tried to stand up, grunting with pain. The woman helped him up, then gestured for the others to bring the suit to him rather than ask him to walk to the suit. There was another man lying on tarpaulins. Covington recognized him as the man he had thrown at the crewman. Covington straightened a little, remembering the others' courage.

With much help from several men, and much pain, Covington managed to slide into the red suit. With the help of the powered actuators, he was able to stand unsteadily by himself, but when he tried to move he lost all coordination and would have fallen if the others had not caught him.

"Relax as well as you can," the voice of the Hands said quietly. They raised the volume and addressed the people around him. "Please carry Sad For Brian up to the bulkhead door. Don't jostle him more than you can help."

They lifted him gently and carried him up the ramp to the door, but every movement hurt. "Stand him up directly in front of the door, please," the Hands said. "There is nothing to provide traction here, so you all will have to get behind Sad For Brian and brace him as well as you can."

When they were arranged as strongly as possible behind his back, the Hands said to Covington, "You will need to kick the door in. The suit has enough power to do this, but you must supply the initial motor impulse to start the leg moving."

"Can you change the power setting to move really fast?" Covington said. "Because I couldn't kick my way out of a wet paper bag right now."

"We can. Don't be startled by the disproportionate movement."

Covington faced the door, leaned backward slightly against the crowd behind him and gingerly swung his left foot forward at the door. He tried to be prepared, but was still taken by surprise when his foot rocketed forward and slammed thunderously into the metal bulkhead door. Pain from his shoulder dazzled him.

"Again," the Hands said. Covington weakly moved his leg and his armored foot crashed the door another time.

"Again."

On the fifth kick the bulkhead door gave way. The panicky crewman fired instantly with his rifle and the bullet rang against Covington's suit and knocked him backward. The people behind him picked him up, pointed his feet forward and ran toward the crewman, using Covington as a battering ram. The crewman went down in a heap, and the battle was over.

The Hands were already issuing orders to the people when Covington fell back into unconsciousness.

He woke in a hospital, under blankets and with a soft hat on his head. He had a short, itchy beard. The hospital was crude and cheap to his eyes, accustomed to the hospitals he knew, but the atmosphere was unmistakable. He was lying on a cot in a large open room filled with beds, looking up at a ceiling of beams and wooden planks. There was no monitoring equipment, no nurse call button, no electronic beeping. But there was a pretty nurse in an odd hat next to him, smiling with reassurance.

"Good morning!" she said. "I'm Medical Society Suriah, you're on the planet Sallin Hoor Martinam, which is one of the human planets in Home space, and you're okay. The Hands told us how to treat you, and you're getting better fast. They also said you'd want to know right away that everybody on the ship is okay, and that Brythe has not had an eruption, whatever that means. How do you feel?"

Covington took inventory. "Actually, I'm fine," he said. "No pain, nothing. How long have I been here?"

"It's been eight days. The Hands sent us some good medicine for you," Medical Society Suriah said. "We have also patched up your suit with parts they sent us. It's right over there."

The red suit was standing by itself, cleaned up and with the helmet repaired or replaced. "Good morning," the Hands said through the outside speaker.

"I need to get back to Brythe," Covington said.

"We anticipated this," the Hands said. "The outside ship you came in has been modified so that you can operate it by yourself, and you can go back to pick up another load of refugees."

"How's the stop-relying-on-the-Hands-of-God thing working out for you?"

"That is a long-term plan," the Hands said. "There may be local exceptions during the process."

"Glad to hear you're on it. Yeah, if I'm all patched up then let's get back to Brythe. I've got relatives there."

"You have. All men are related."

"Ooh, that's heavy! You guys have got this preacher act really *down*, you know?"

Chapter 21

New Town had had four churches, of which two were left standing, and at least thirty taverns, many of which were still in operation even after their buildings had tumbled down. The tremors were coming two and three times a day now.

Wiegand and Indarya stood before a bar called, in Brythean fashion, "Drunk and Rowdy". They had previously visited, that day, bars called "Punch Them All Out," "Window Breakers" and "Flat on the Floor." In truth, the people of New Town did not really drink to excess very often, but considered it jolly to pretend otherwise.

This particular wooden building was leaning and the windows were piles of shattered glass on the ground, but the bar was doing a good business inside.

"Okay, are we ready for another batch of stick-in-the-muds?" Wiegand said.

"I *am* ready," Indarya said. "You know, I can do this. I never found anything I was really good at before, but I'm getting pretty good at preaching to guys in bars."

"You've got what it takes," Wiegand said. "Being a pretty woman helps, of course. The guys sure don't pay as much attention to me. But besides that, you can catch them and hold them. Not everybody's got that talent."

"Thanks! Also thanks for being my body guard, I really appreciate that."

"Hey, I started out as a dishwasher and now I've been promoted to bouncer," Wiegand said. "It's the advantage of a university education, of course. I'll go in first. It's show time."

They walked in. It was dim inside and crowded, with men and women sitting at tables and standing in the aisles. The bartender was busily pouring drinks which were carried to the patrons by his three small children.

Indarya pushed herself into the middle of the room. "Hi, everybody!" she said loudly. "My name is Not Yet Indarya and I'm here to tell you there are going to be three more evacuation ships coming into port in about two hours from now, and all you folks need to get on them BECAUSE THE WHOLE PLANET IS GOING TO BLOW UP! You, your house, this bar, your kids — blooey! I don't know how to say it any plainer than that."

"What kind of a stupid name is that?" somebody yelled.

"It means I have to get a new affiliation, because I used to be Sad For Indarya but Sad For is falling to pieces, in case you have haven't noticed. I'm going to another planet where I'll be safe and you should, too."

"You from the government? Or the church or something?"

"I'm from the government *and* the church. We've got to get everybody off the planet within a couple of days and we're out talking to you folks that haven't left yet."

"To hell with you!" a woman yelled. "The Hands of God are going to fix it. Haven't you seen what they're building down there? You're just trying to get our houses, or something."

"Nobody wants *your* house, Bunch of Winos Opella," another woman yelled out. "Your house has bugs!" There was general laughter and the two women jumped out of their chairs to glare at each other. Indarya nimbly snatched the woman's chair and pulled it out to stand on it.

A man near the wall said, "Look, nobody pays much attention to Sad For Opella but she's right. We've got a problem and the Hands are going to fix it, the way they always do."

"Talk to me," Indarya said, taking in everyone with a gesture of her arms. "The Hands are sure enough building *something*, but this has never happened to any planet before and they can't possibly have any experience with this. If that machine doesn't work perfectly the very first time, there won't be a second time and You. Will. Be. Dead! So do you trust the Hands that much? Who here trusts them like that?"

Voices rose throughout the room. "I heard the Hands are, like, little animals," a voice said.

"Yeah, I heard that, too," somebody else said. "And anyway, the Hands aren't here. It's the Cortays that are building that thing, and I know damn well *they* can make mistakes."

"The Hands are smart enough to make sure the Cortays don't cause problems. Besides, if you go get on their ship, *that* was made by Cortays."

"I ain't goin'," an old man said. "Anybody that thinks a planet can blow up is just ignorant. That ain't gonna happen. You people are fools." He drank a long draft of his beer.

"Why does the government want us out of here anyway?" another voice asked. "Something's going on here."

"And I stopped believing anything the church said a long time ago. Like about the time I learned to walk!"

"There will be an explosion bigger than anything you can imagine," Indarya said earnestly. "We don't know where it will happen but it doesn't matter, because the shock will run all over this planet. There will be fires and floods and rocks falling from the sky, and everything that *can* burn *will* burn, and then a cloud of dust will hide the light from the sky for a thousand days or more. No crops will grow. Nobody will survive. Believe me, if the Hands are successful you can come back. But right now you've got to go."

"Why would they bring us back? That costs money," somebody asked.

Wiegand stepped up. "Yeah, I wondered about that too," he said. "Turns out some smart guy on Home had the idea that if the whole planet gets shaken up, it'll open up lots of veins of minerals and ores they can mine. I suppose he's right. It won't be for couple-thousand days, though."

"What are we going to do to make a living in the mean time?"

"We'll work it out," Indarya said. "Honest, the church and the government on Home and the Hands are all working on how to handle all the people coming to other planets. But you have to leave here, you can't stay."

"I don't know if I want the Hands' help," a woman said. "I hear bad things."

"Yeah," Indarya said with exasperation, "the Hands decided we need to stop depending on them so much, and maybe we do, and *they* started all those stories you've heard. They think this is the perfect time for us to learn to depend on ourselves. What a bunch of jerks! Anyway, what I'm trying to say is, we're working on it and we'll take care of you."

"You're crazy!" another woman yelled, with many supporting cat-calls from the crowd. "There've been earthquakes before. This will go away, and if any of you leave, the rest of us who stayed here, we're not going to let you back! This is OUR planet!"

A private fist-fight erupted in the back of the room, and within a few minutes had spread throughout the bar. "Let's get out of here," Wiegand said to Indarya, who was watching, wide-eyed. He helped her off the chair, punched back at a man who attacked him and dragged her to the door. They fled outside.

"I should've worn the power suit," Wiegand said. "Wow, that was the worst yet."

"If we'd walked in wearing those big suits," Indarya said, "they'd have ganged up on us, first thing."

"I guess you're right. Look, I can't take any more bars today. Let's get back downtown."

"Okay. I guess some of them will come around. My God, Pete, people are going to die here because they're hard-headed."

"People die of that all the time," Wiegand said. "You do what you can. Don't blame yourself."

They walked back toward the main church downtown, which was also now the headquarters of the city government and the evacuation command. The streets were nearly empty. Evacuation ships had been coming for several days, some volunteered by Cortays, some chartered by the church and Home government.

There were also ships run by Vallow's countrymen, of the same cubical shape as the slave-traders who had carried off Covington and a hundred or more townspeople. Sani had had to get the priest, God Nanhallit, to come to the spaceport and give his approval before anyone would get aboard the new ships.

Vallow, his leg in a cast and still shaky from the attack, translated for the ships' crews, collected a just-barely-reasonable fare from each passenger and kept a commission for himself. He was getting moderately rich while personally saving at least a fifth of the population of Brythe.

The church building was visibly cracked on one brick wall but still in relatively sound shape. Most of the church volunteers and government people had already left, but those remaining were bustling, taking care of details of the evacuation and filling out the inevitable paperwork required in even the most dire situations.

Nightfall happened to catch them as they entered. Wiegand and Indarya found blankets and huddled up in a corner of the building. They slept in each other's arms.

In the morning they were met by the priest, God Nanhallit. He was weary and unshaven, making a hasty breakfast from fruit and bread, which he also offered to them.

"Is Sani here?" Indarya asked.

"No, she's out in the village of Lodd, trying to convince the farmers out there, same kind of thing you've been doing. She was here trying to work on the bookkeeping for this scramble, but losing Sad For Brian hit her pretty hard."

"Us, too," Wiegand said.

"I'm sorry, I really am. A terrible thing. Anyway, I told her to go out and do something else. But listen, can you help me out with another job?"

"We're here to work," Wiegand said. "What do you need?"

"Remember your buddy Gron Orrata Hemmet Card, the teacher?" Nanhallit asked.

"Sure. We saw him the other day down by the spaceport, yelling at a crowd."

"He's been attracting bigger and bigger crowds," Nanhallit said. "We're worried about what he might do. Would you and Indarya go down there and see if you can talk sense to them? I don't want you to get hurt. Put on your big suits."

"I guess so," Indarya said. "You think they'll listen to us?"

"If not," Nanhallit said, "use the suits and try to prevent them from hurting anybody else. From what I hear, he's getting 'em pretty worked up."

"Okay. You going to be all right here?"

"The Hands say we have about another two days yet, depending on how long the days are."

Wiegand and Indarya found their powered suits, which they had stored in the church building, and took off at an easy run toward the spaceport. Long before they reached it, they could see the Hands' machine being constructed by Cortay workmen. It was huge and getting bigger, rising far above New Town and thrusting massive metal roots deep into the ground. More Cortay ships carrying construction materials arrived every day. Many of them carried passengers on the trip out, to be delivered to other human planets.

The machine was so inhuman in shape and construction that it was hard to look at. It leaned, with a vague suggestion of a cresting wave or toppling mountain. It was mostly green in color, but shot through with yellow and white streaks. Lamps of all colors, placed irregularly, lit it with garish spots. It had holes they could see through, catwalks and balconies, drooping cables and rotating antennas. Cortay workmen crawled over it, looking tiny.

"It sure looks like it ought to work," Indarya said, pointing across the river to the machine.

"How do you mean?"

"Well, it just looks — I don't know, big and really scientific and all alien and powerful, I guess."

"I wouldn't be surprised," Wiegand said, "if the actual working part of that monster was the size of a deck of cards."

"Why would they make it so big, then?"

"To be impressive, I guess. Why would they make it at all? Maybe the Hands are sincere in wanting to save the planet and maybe they can do it. Or maybe they want you to think they're trying to save the planet but they're incompetent, which helps with their plan to wean humans off reliance on the

Hands. Or maybe they never intended it to work because they calculated they need to kill a bunch of people to deliver a big enough shock, to get, you know, the greatest good for the greatest number. Hell, maybe we're just not smart enough to understand the reason."

"Well, aren't you little Mr. Cheerful," Indarya said. "Look, I'm the one who's losing my home. You don't even live here, really."

"No, guess I don't," Wiegand said. "I suppose another planet will be just as good as this one. I wish Brian was with me, though."

Indarya was instantly contrite. "Oh, God, Pete, I'm so sorry," she said.

"It's okay," Wiegand said. "Let's go listen in on Card. He always wanted to lecture to more students, I think."

Chapter 22

Card stood before the crowd on the periphery of the spaceport, standing on two wooden boxes. The construction being completed at the direction of the Hands of God was behind him where the people could see it.

Card did not look like a fiery orator. He looked nervous and shy, twisting his hands and fidgeting. He was plump and middle-aged and ordinary, but he had the knack of keeping the people's attention. He said this:

My name is Sad For Card. Yeah, I know, some of you knew me by another name. That was in my past

235

life, long ago — fifteen days or more. [A little laughter.]

I used to be a snob. Really, I was. Back then, I would never have tried to talk to you because I thought I was better than you. Now, it's still hard for me to talk to you because you mean so much to me, because I love you all. [Laughter] You're right to laugh, you know. It's funny, it's a joke. My head almost wound up facing the wrong way, I turned around so fast.

The truth will do that to you. I learned the truth.

That ... that *thing* you're looking at behind me, that's not the truth. It's a lie, the whole phony "machine" and everything the so-called Hands of God told you about it, all false, all fake, all meant for your destruction.

Yes, your destruction! Your *death*, you and your wives and husbands and children. Not a clean death, either. A dirty, painful death. That's what the Hands' lies are intended for.

The ships those other fools are getting on, those are lies, too. The planet is not blowing up because — you know this! — *things like that don't really happen*, do they? The Hands just want you off the planet, and they don't care how.

But you don't have to fall for those lies! You don't have to die, you don't have to leave!

I don't want you to die. Who would ... what human being would ever want that? Of course no human would, because we are *human*. That's what human beings do, we take care of each other. It's our pride and our glory. I don't want you to have to give up your home, your family, the places you love.

What would the "Hands of God" ever know about any of that?

Hold fast to the truth! That's what will protect you! And I'm here to tell you the truth, not because there's anything special about me but because I happened to find out about it, and because I want you to be safe and happy just like any decent human would.

When I was young I used to wonder if God really loved me. I saw how many, many people in the world there were, and I thought that God couldn't possibly know and love all of us. But now I know.

I know that it's even worse than that.

A million times worse, a trillion times worse — there are no words for how many humans and other kinds of people there are. Listen to me, look into your hearts, tell me if you don't feel it's true: this world is only the tiniest part of a world so much greater the imagination can't encompass it. Brythe and Home and all the other planets we know of are not a tenth of a tenth of a tenth of all the inhabited worlds there are.

And you haven't tasted the bitter dregs of that idea yet, because it gets still worse.

Our world, and all the worlds you have ever heard of or imagined, are only particles making up a greater world. All of us together are not even the relative size of a grain of sand in a child's sand castle on the beach. If you think of God as that child, cheerfully making His creations out of the sand, then you can understand that we, all of us, are about as important to God as one grain of that sand.

You think God loves you? He might love one of the creatures of that larger world, I wouldn't know. I do know He can't squint His eyes tight enough to see something as small as you or me. You know that too, if you search your own heart. You've always known it. You feel alone, you always have.

You know who loves you? I do. [Laughs.]

Yeah, it's not worth much. You were hoping for a better-looking guy, you ladies, right? You men, you were hoping for somebody richer, right? [Laughs.]

Still, as bad and small as my love is, you can have it. I hope to have *your* love in return, I hope to earn it and deserve it. Might take a while, of course, because for most of you, I'm just some nut standing on a box shouting. That's okay, I can accept that. I'm new at this.

But think about the people you *do* love. Your family, your friends, your affiliate group, your neighbors. Whoever you are, whatever your situation in life, I'll bet there's *somebody* you love, who loves you. Am I wrong?

Love is what is fundamental to the world! Not matter, not government, not the Hands for damn sure. Love is the building block of which the world is really made. I don't mean some watery imaginary "love" the priest tells you about, not some abstraction dreamed up by the Hands, but real love of one human for another. Love for people you can see and touch, that's the reality.

That's the *truth*, and you know I'm right, don't you?

There's other kinds of love. Love can be bad. You can fool yourself — not all of the loves you think you have are real. I used to think I loved beer, and then I found that when I had real love, love for all of you, I could give up the beer without a thought. I used to think I loved learning, but now I see how empty that is. Only people matter.

I used to think I didn't love this town, and this planet. But now I know I do, and I think you do, too. I love Sad For! I love Brythe! [Cheers]

People, we've got to look out for each other, because for damn sure nobody else is going to do it. Not God, He barely knows we exist. Not the church, not the companies on Home who built the factories here, not the government on Home.

And definitely not the Hands!

You've felt the ground shake. In fact, it happened again just this morning. Scared me as bad as anybody, I'll tell you. Now look over there at the machine the Hands are building.

Does that look like something that would help you? Does that look like a loving present? Or does it look like something you'd see in a nightmare?

That machine is not there to stop the earthquakes. I tell you it's there to *make* the earthquakes! I think the Hands have other machines, and we've been feeling the ground move when they work. But this one's the kick in the teeth that will take the town of Sad For completely out, because it's right here.

Now why would the Hands of God want to get humans off of Brythe, dead or alive?

Look who's getting on those ships.

All the good little church folks, the ones who listen to whatever the priest says. All the kids, who don't know what's going on but have to follow their parents. All the herd-people, the followers, the ones who will let themselves be led around by the nose. *That's* who's on those ships.

Look at the ones left behind. Look around you at your neighbors here, listening to me. What's different about us? Why are we *here* and the credulous fools are *there*?

Because we know the truth. We know that Brythe is important because it's important to *us*, not because God cares one way or the other. We know that people are important because they're important to *us*, not to some un-human big brains who keep us as a hobby.

Make no mistake. *You* are not getting on one of those ships because the Hands don't want *you* spreading the truth to other people on other planets. *You* are marked for death by earthquakes.

And it's because you know the truth. But the truth will save you even when as puts you in danger, because we are *humans* and we can *act*.

We can act *now*!

Are you with me? Will you act today to save your own city, your own world? Will you join us to cry, We Are Important! Will you show your love for your family, for your world, for the person standing next to you?

There is the machine meant to destroy you. *There* is the engine the Liars of God want to use on you. *There* is your death — unless you join with us now!

Now!

Now!

Chapter 23

As Indarya and Wiegand watched, the mob broke and ran toward the Hands' machine. There were hundreds in the crowd, with Card puffing and running in the center. The fence was topped with barbed wire: the people in the vanguard threw themselves across it and the others stepped on their backs until the fence could be pulled down completely.

Cortay workmen sprinted away from them, dropping their tools in panic. The tools were picked up in moments, and the mob was instantly armed with clubs and sharp-pointed weapons.

They overran the anti-gravity lifters and in a few moments more, the air was full of gliding, colliding shapes as the untrained pilots attempted to deliver loads of rioters to balconies on the machine high above the ground.

A voice spoke inside both Indarya's and Wiegand's helmets. "We are the Hands of God," it said. "Please help us. You must protect the machine."

"I figured you guys were listening in," Wiegand said. "Is the machine real? Or are you just trying to protect your image?"

"The machine is real," the Hands said, "and it controls powerful energies, powerful enough to affect all of the nucleons that compose the planet. It is not yet completed, and some of the regulating systems are not in place. If they turn the machine on, the consequences will be bad."

"What do you want us to do?" Indarya asked.

"Please look near the top of the machine. There is a balcony there with a small door. This is the main control room. You must use the powered suits to get there and disable it. No one must operate the controls inside."

Wiegand sighed. "Okay," he said. "Indarya, I hate to involve you in this but we've got to work together. Can we get one of those flying fork-lift things to take us up to the top?"

They ran straight toward the machine, trusting the rioters to get out of their way. "I'm with you, dear," Indarya said. "These jerks don't have any idea how to use these lifters. We'll catch one when he flies low."

The lifters were reeling and pitching above them. Some of the hysterical operators had fallen off already, and Wiegand saw a pilotless lifter spiral down and smash into the side of the Hands' machine, cracking open a dozen panels. There were more mysterious colored lights on the inside.

A lifter swooped over Indarya's head. With the power of the armored suit, she leaped up, grabbed the frame and with no hesitation punched out the wailing man trying to fly it. He tumbled to the ground and she immediately straightened out the lifter, piloted it in a smooth circle and landed it neatly in front of Wiegand. "Get on the front and hold on," she said.

"You can fly one of these?"

"Sure. I used to have a pretty good factory job running one of these."

"How come you were pushing a broom in the sawmill?" Wiegand asked thoughtlessly, lying down on the fork at the front and grabbing the bars with his armored gloves.

"I got fired for drinking on the job," Indarya said. The lifter swung up into the air, avoiding a posse of rioters running toward them. "It's okay, I'm straight now."

"I didn't know that," Wiegand said lamely.

"Pete, I've decided I'm going to keep you," Indarya said. "So you'll get to know a whole bunch of things about me. You keep asking questions like that you'll find out some stuff about me you really don't want to know." Under Indarya's piloting, the lifter soared up and came to a precise stop a few inches away from the balcony the Hands had pointed out.

Wiegand pulled himself clumsily onto the balcony and stood. Indarya was a foot away, standing on the operator's deck at the back of the bobbing lifter. Wiegand held out his gloved and armored hand and Indarya touched it with her metal glove. She smiled for him inside her helmet. "Indarya," Wiegand said, "I'm ... yeah ... oh, God ... yes. Yes. I'll make a better speech later."

"I know you will," she said. "You go inside. I'm going to fly around and try to pick some of these fools off the machine." She pulled her hand back, tilted the lifter and sailed away, slanting downward.

"Please enter the control room," the Hands said in Wiegand's ear. He spent a moment vainly peering out to try to see Indarya, then opened the door and squeezed through the small doorway.

The floor shuddered momentarily. "Another earthquake?" Wiegand asked.

"Not yet. One is coming shortly," the Hands said. "This disturbance is because some of Card's people have set off explosives."

"Where did they get those?"

"Card made bombs in his chemistry lab," the Hands said. "Please kneel down and look underneath the panel. You can turn on an outside light on your helmet with the switch on the ring where the helmet is joined to the suit. Good. Please grab the red cylinder you see by your left hand, and pull it out. You will have to break the wires it is connected to." Wiegand did this. The cylinder was the size and color he imagined a stick of dynamite would be, and he handled it gingerly.

"Good. That disables all controls in this room," the Hands said. "The rioters cannot operate the machine now."

"Are you going to have time to rebuild all this before the eruption?" Wiegand asked.

"We hope so. The time of the eruption is not precisely determined. Will you climb down now and get everyone off the machine before they damage it more severely?"

"Sure." Wiegand got to his feet and stepped back out onto the little balcony. He was four or five stories above the ground, which was thick with screaming rioters. Card's attack apparently had attracted an even larger crowd from the group along the spaceport fences. They were clanging tools against the side of the machine, climbing up the ladders and stairs and quarreling with each other.

Close up, the Hands' machine was even more repulsive than when seen from a distance. The walls were crusty and rough with what looked like applied printed circuits. Incomprehensible mechanisms poked out randomly, and the colored lights blinked in rippling patterns that made Wiegand queasy.

There was a ladder fixed to the outside next to the control room, and he swung onto it, unhappy with his clumsiness and weight in the bulky armor. He lumbered down the ladder until it reached another balcony, at one end of an open corridor that went all the way through the structure. Wiegand searched it quickly and found no one, although the sound of voices and banging came from a level below. There were no ladders or stairs going downward from this position on either side of the machine. He did find a metal cable that was loose on one end and attached somewhere unseen at the other. He pulled on it lightly, trying not to use the power of the suit, and wondered if it would hold him. He was looking downward from the balcony on the far side when a silent attacker rushed up behind him and pushed him over.

He clutched the metal cable and his armored, powered gloves clamped onto it. Wiegand tumbled over the edge, looking back at the laughing face of the man who had pushed him, and swung like a wrecking ball at the end of the cable. He crashed into the machine's wall with his shoulder and the panel crumpled. He fell twenty feet or more to the floor of a room the size of an auditorium and filled with hulking shapes of machinery colored in deep purples and greens. He was not hurt much inside the suit, but he could not regain his feet: the floor was shaking.

"This will be a major earthquake," the voice of the Hands told him calmly. "Can you get out of this room?"

"Not sure." Wiegand looked up. There were plain white lights on the high ceiling of the room. He looked up when some of the lights went out, and saw the ceiling flexing and cracking. As he watched, it tore open and with a terrible noise another huge machine fell through from the room above. Twenty or more people fell with it, screaming.

The falling intruder tumbled into the machines already in the room, and the people falling with it were knocked cruelly into the floor, the other machinery and each other. Some were bleeding freely, and some were already dead. Wiegand started forward to try to pull out one man who slid under a block of metal tipped precariously against another piece, ready to fall in a moment, but the man looked at his huge, red, inhuman form and screamed. Wiegand backed off, unable to reason or decide what to do. The room was still shaking.

A low-pitched drone filled the room, quickly rising in pitch until it was a frantic high whistle. A monstrous purple machine, reaching floor to ceiling, had turned itself on. Lights ran along the surface and the top rotated.

"Peter, you must leave now if you can. No one else can be helped. You must get outside as quickly as possible," the voice of the Hands said.

"What is that machine doing?"

"It cannot be explained quickly, but it results in channeling the power of this earthquake into such a narrow channel that it is cracking the surface of the planet. The electron emission will happen *here* because of this crust rupture, although it would not have happened here otherwise. It will happen within minutes. You must leave. We are notifying Indarya as well. The Cortays will leave on their own ship. Please, Peter, go now."

Wiegand looked left and right at the injured rioters, deeply conflicted, but one of them decided the issue for him by raising a gun. He aimed at Wiegand, his eyes mad. Wiegand leaped up the trembling wall, clawing at various fixtures and cables until he was able to pull himself through the hole he had made falling in. A shot pierced the wall as he pulled himself halfway out.

Indarya was there with the lifter. Wiegand leaped onto it, grabbing desperately at the fork, and as soon as he was able to hold on, she tilted the lifter away from the structure. The whine of the operating component was still loud.

Wiegand was facing down. He stared in horror and cried, "Indarya! Look! Look down!"

The ground was heaving like a boiling liquid. A crack started at the base of the Hands' machine, from which four tremendous metal roots went deep into the ground. A canyon ripped open and the land split in two, with New Town and the spaceport on one side, farmers' fields on the other.

The canyon gaped wider and wider, cascades of rock and soil sliding into it, and the far side pulled away with sickening speed. The canyon was miles long already and the end was beyond sight. As Wiegand and Indarya watched, their thoughts frozen, the crack reached a mile into the ground.

A mile of ground was all there was. At the bottom of the canyon, the sides peeled away to show featureless blackness.

Under the thinnest of skins of rock and soil, the interior of the planet Brythe was a black emptiness, filled with protons and neutrons that had no visible structure beyond twinkles of light here and there. It was not space, it was not matter in any sense they could understand, it was not nothing. Brythe was a bubble of landscape enclosing a sphere that was outside all human experience.

The machine tilted. If it made a noise, they could not hear it through the air-filling roar already present. The machine teetered and rocked, then slowly pitched forward and fell into the canyon. Wriggling human bodies leaped from it and fell at the same slow-seeming rate. The machine dwindled to nothing and vanished into the interior.

"Go to the spaceport," the voice of the Hands said to them. They both turned, unable to watch the alien spectacle a moment longer, and saw a cubical spaceship, white with a design of green stripes, settling to the ground.

"It's the slavers! They've come back," Indarya said.

"It is Brian Covington," the Hands said. "Go there now. You have about nine minutes to leave this area before the ship will be caught in the shockwave."

Indarya turned her clumsy craft toward the spaceport. Behind them, the black interior of Brythe flashed into a gathering white light which fanned upward from the canyon.

Chapter 24

Vallow had been at the spaceport, supervising the loading of a ship. At the Hands' urgent message, he had sent it flying low over the city to pick up as many as possible from the city center. He himself was asked by the Hands to remain to wait for Covington's ship, which was just reaching the ground when Indarya flew in with the lifter, Wiegand clinging to the fork.

Covington had both doors of the bridge airlock open a few seconds after the ship touched ground. Vallow clambered in first, hampered by the cast on his leg. "I'm a trained pilot," he gasped. "I can fly this better than you can taking orders from the Hands. We've got to go."

"You got it," Covington said. "The ground's ripping *right here?*"

"I guess. The big machine the Hands were building just fell in. I don't know what happened."

Indarya jumped in, her bulky powered suit forcing Covington to stand back from the inside door. Wiegand followed a moment later.

"I'm glad you're okay," Wiegand said, tearing off his helmet. "Tell me later. We've gotta smoke here."

"Where is Sani?" Covington demanded.

"The village of Lodd," Indarya said. "I can get us there if you fly low so I can see the road."

"Vallow, take it," Covington said.

"Hang on. I'm going to have to turn the internal gravity off to maneuver," Vallow said. He stood before the control panel, moving his hands precisely. The ship lifted, tipped and traveled away from the city as fast as Vallow dared go horizontally. Indarya called out directions, making a mistake once and correcting herself immediately.

In less than three minutes they found the village, a little cluster of wooden houses surrounded by fields. No one was in the street that ran down the middle, so Vallow parked the ship there. Covington was out the airlock door instantly, running for the schoolhouse where Indarya assured him meetings would be held. "Open the cargo doors," he yelled behind him.

He burst through the door to face a meeting of perhaps ten farm families, with Sani facing them. Sani screamed, and he yelled "I'm okay, I'll tell you later. Everybody out! We've got to go! It's starting!"

The small crowd erupted into shouts and screams. Covington grabbed Sani by the wrist and pulled her outside. "Folks," he yelled, "we're leaving right now. Get aboard or get left behind!"

Covington and Sani ran for the bridge airlock. Her hat blew off and she turned to chase it, until Covington spun her around and pushed her through the door. Fifteen or twenty people ran into the cargo hold while the others hesitated and dithered. "Take her up!" Covington yelled. Vallow lifted the ship into the air even as the cargo doors were closing.

"One minute," the voice of the Hands said.

"Will it take some time for the explosion to get here?" Sani asked breathlessly, clutching Covington.

"Almost none. The shockwave travels at the speed of sound."

"Vallow, can you let me talk to the people in the cargo hold?" Covington asked. Vallow flipped a switch and Covington yelled, "Everybody in the ship! There are a lot of ropes still down there. Tie yourselves to the wall. We're going to get knocked around. Right now!"

"Okay, group hug, everybody," Wiegand said. "Indarya, we've got the armor so we're on the outside. Vallow, you stay at the controls. Brian, Sani, put your backs to him so he doesn't get thrown around. Indarya and I will grab on to the console and each other with the suit grippers. Hold on tight."

The ship rose at the best speed Vallow could coax out of it. The shockwave caught them while they were low enough to still see the roads and fields around New Town through the window on the bridge. The ship was tumbled like a die thrown over a gambling table. The shock whirled them miles to the side through the air, the view spinning so rapidly they were sick with vertigo.

Vallow was able to keep his place in front of the controls, braced against the others. He dared not apply thrust until he could keep the ship pointed in one direction. He worked the controls as well as he could in the maddening spin. When the initial shock had passed over them, he was able to slow the spinning until he had the ship pointed away from the ground, and with no more aim than that sent it surging above the atmosphere.

Brythe was a blue arc below them when Vallow relaxed. "The shock can't get out of the atmosphere," he said. "We're safe now, if the hull hasn't been cracked. He consulted more of his instruments, looking for leaks. Wiegand and Indarya let go of their grip on the console (they had left crumples in the metal) and Covington and Sani turned to look outside.

The electron was long gone, moving at relativistic speeds. Its passage was marked by a vertical column of clouds and dust reaching to the top of the stratosphere, spreading at several separate levels into a mushroom shape.

The shockwave was a foaming ring, miles high and hundreds of miles wide, expanding as they watched. Everything inside the ring was hidden by clouds of dust. There was no trace left of New Town.

They watched silently as the shockwave expanded across the continent that had held New Town. It showed no signs of weakening.

"Hands," Indarya said quietly, "how many died?"

"Nine hundred and twenty," the Hands said, using the outside speaker of her suit. "All the rest have been evacuated."

"Nine hundred and twenty," Sani said. "God, keep them and cherish them."

"We have failed," the Hands said. "We did not anticipate this. All were supposed to have been saved."

"Let's go down into the hold," Sani said. "I'll bet some of those people are hurting."

"I'll be along in a minute," Covington said. "Vallow, you okay here?"

"I'm fine for the present," Vallow said. "I'm sorry for your world, and all those people."

"Yeah," Covington said. "Not my world, I guess, but definitely my people. I'm going to go into the little corridor over there for a while and pray."

"Come help us when you can," Wiegand said. They left for the cargo hold, and Covington pulled his armored suit into the corridor and sat on the floor with his head in his hands, praying, sometimes aloud and sometimes in his mind.

After a long time, he slapped his hand against the suit. "Well," he said, "what have you guys got to say for yourselves?"

"We have failed," the Hands repeated. "We did not expect that irrational reaction to our plan to make men less dependent on us. We did not allow for the possibility that our machine could be powered-on without the controls. We did not love your people well enough to protect them all. Humans have died, and it is our fault. We are filled with self-loathing and sorrow. We stand convicted of sin before God, horrible sin. We ..."

"Oh, give it a rest!" Convington said in exasperation, and quoted, "Brother, you ain't confessin', you's braggin'!"

The Hands were uncharacteristically silent for a long moment. "We *were* enjoying the emotion of guilt," they said at last. "We apologize for that as well. We have no experience handling emotions of this kind."

"Seriously? You've been the super-duper angels of God to the humans, and to the Cortays for a couple-three hundred years and you're *just now* learning what sin means?"

"Up until now, we have been right about everything."

Covington shook his head and smiled in spite of himself. "You guys are a real piece of work, you know that?"

"Your meaning is unclear."

"Meaning is allowed to be that," Covington said. "You guys need to go away and work on your own problems for a human generation or two. Also, you need to shut up."

Sani came back into the corridor. "Brian, can you come down and help out? A lot of people got banged up down there."

"Sure thing," he said. "I'm here to help."

Epilogue

Two young women, both wearing white lab coats, stepped gingerly into the second-floor lab that had been occupied by Peter Wiegand, Brian Covington and the Dense Memory Device. One of them glanced at the instrument the other held in her hand. "A geiger counter?" she asked.

"I grabbed it off the bench," she said. "Just figured I'd better check."

"There aren't supposed to be any radioactives anywhere on the second floor."

"Whatever happened here, wasn't supposed to happen, either." She pointed the wand toward the sunny windows, the equipment surrounding the empty spot where the DMD had been, the benches. There were only a few clicks from it. "Just background levels," she said. "Whatever it was, it didn't throw off any radiation."

"But," the other said, "where *are* those two guys? We saw them run in the door not a minute ago, and the windows are still closed. How did they get out?"

"I don't know."

The electron from Brythe happened to pass through the detector tube of the geiger counter. It made a sound: *click.*